A "Blue" For Illi

OTHER BOOKS

BY

Nancy Hartwell

SHOESTRING THEATER

GABRIELLA

WHO WAS SYLVIA?

A "Blue" For Illi

by

NANCY HARTWELL (Pseud.)

Claire Wallis Callahan

Illustrated by

DON SIBLEY

HENRY HOLT AND COMPANY · NEW YORK

Library of Congress Catalog Card Number: 54-5738

In Canada, George J. McLeod, Ltd.

Published, April, 1954
Second Printing, September, 1954
Third Printing, March, 1955
Fourth Printing, October, 1957

93495-0414

Printed in the United States of America

FOR THE

de Lamos Family

WHO HAVE BEEN SO GENEROUS

WITH THEIR HELP AND FRIENDSHIP

A "Blue" For Illi

Chapter 1

*T*HERE WAS the first nip of fall in the air that October afternoon.

"Real football weather," Geegee Fairchild said to Illi, who was waiting at the bus stop in front of the Waverly High School. Geegee, whose real name was Georgiana, lived for the week-end games and would rather take a chance on walking home than miss the afternoon practice scrimmage.

"I'm going to wait to watch the team practice," she continued. "Why don't you stay? You'd enjoy it, Illi. I might be able to give you a lift home. I'll call my mother and ask her to pick us up with the car."

"I am sorry, but I must hurry," Illi said in her precise

1

English that had a slight foreign accent combined with a Southern drawl. "The football is not so important to me."

"But you'd love it—once you understood it."

"I am sure that I would," Illi said with the politeness for which she had already earned a reputation. "Thank you for asking me."

"I suppose it's your—well, whatever Ardis is to you, isn't it?" she asked carelessly, her eyes on the gym door.

Illi nodded. "She expects me," she said. "I cannot disappoint her."

"I suppose not," Geegee agreed. "I liked Ardis when I met her the other day. She's fun in spite of her trouble. I always used to think invalids were grouchy or else sickeningly cheerful. But your Ardis isn't at all. She's—regular."

"Yes," Illi said, "she is—how do you say *wunderbar?* —wonderful."

"Well, give her my love. See you tomorrow." Geegee moved off as two padded figures ran out the gym door to join the others on the field.

The bus drew up and Illi, edging to the curb, jumped on first. She always did this so she could get her favorite seat just behind the driver. She didn't notice the looks exchanged behind her back by the half-dozen other boys and girls who followed her. What one wanted one had to take, was Illi's motto; one had to fight for the good things of this world. Not that she was rude about it, but over the hard years she had learned all the little tricks of getting along in a selfish, fighting world.

She sat down and opened a book to read during the ride out to the Enwright place just four miles from town. It was a luxury to ride such a short distance. Over there in Europe she had walked much farther just for a loaf of bread, and hard black bread at that. Everything was so easy in America.

She was the only one to drop off the bus at the foot of the road that led back to some scattered houses. The voices of her classmates followed her.

"Bye, Illi!"

"See you tomorrow!"

"Don't study too hard."

She stood watching the bus pull away and amble down the road like a fat old hen, taking the careless voices and the bright faces of the boys and girls with it. Standing there in the typical American countryside, she looked like any American girl in her pleated plaid skirt, tan sweater set, and loafers. But inside she did not feel so. Those boys and girls were not unkind, but they didn't like her. She could feel it. They tried to be nice to her because she was new, a stranger, a foreigner, a DP. But they seemed to think she should fall on their necks because America had taken her in and given her a home.

Well, somebody had to give her a home. It was not her fault that she had lost her own, and in Europe there were no homes for the extra people, the homeless. It had to be America, that was so large and so rich and so kind. And, as she had pointed out in history class just today, those first settlers in America, the Pilgrims and all the rest, had come to find new homes away from tyranny. Somebody had laughed when she said this, and she had shut up.

Yes, they meant to be kind to her but they were so—so stupid, so young. They hurt her in so many ways, not intentionally, but because they did not think, and because American boys and girls had a way of making fun of everything. "Kidding" they called it and nobody was supposed to take it seriously. She felt years and years older than the others, even though some of them, all juniors, were her own age, seventeen. She was way ahead of them in everything except English and American history.

In spite of the war and her upset life she had managed to get an education of sorts. There had been periods when she'd studied things the girls and boys over here had never studied. At one time old Mr. Bauer in the bombed-out shelter in Munich had given her a thorough course in astronomy. They would go out at night and study the dark, star-studded sky lying calm and untroubled over the wrecked city, still the same sky that she had seen as a little girl in the peaceful city of Budapest, still the same sky from which the bombers had come during her wanderings, and it would be the same sky a million years from now.

"The world is not topsy-turvy, Illi," old Mr. Bauer had said, "only the people in it, and they will change. You must remember that, child. You are young. You will see better days. But I . . ." he shrugged. Perhaps his luck would not hold out much longer. He was an anti-Nazi, a professor who had been hiding for a long time. A week later the storm troopers came to take him away.

Illi shrugged now, too, as if to toss off her thoughts of Mr. Bauer and all the others who had befriended her and become lost in the awful confusion of war. She must not think of such things. She must think of now and here, and what lay ahead. And she must not stand in the road, dawdling. She must think of Ardis who would be waiting, counting the minutes until Illi came home with the story of the day's happenings.

"You're my daily paper, you know," Ardis would say. "So give me the news, Illi. Tell me about the sports, the fashions, and the society column of Waverly High. How's the football team? What was Geegee wearing today? Have you been asked to sing in the chorus yet?"

And Illi would plop down on the fat hassock beside Ardis' wheel chair and tell her all the things she could remember of the day's doings, before they started the studying which Ardis shared with her. Sometimes she'd illustrate the lessons with funny little sketches to make Ardis laugh—which wasn't hard. Ardis laughed easily. In the few months since she had been part of the Enwright family, Illi had begun to laugh again herself.

She even was able now to tell Ardis some of the things that had happened to her in the past, making them funny rather than tragic. There was the time when someone had stolen her clothes in Augsburg and she had nothing to wear except a discarded trench coat she had found in a ditch. It was buttonless and much too big, but she had cut it down with a razor blade she had found in one pocket and made strips of the left-over cloth. These she tied through slits and the buttonholes to cover her nakedness.

"Once I had to climb a tree to get out of the way of some soldiers and I caught the coat on a branch. The whole thing ripped apart. I had to sit up there and make new holes to put the ties through before I could come down."

She had never thought she could laugh at those things, but here hundreds of miles and several years away they did not seem so important any more. Or maybe it was because she could put them to good use to entertain a girl who was a prisoner, too, a prisoner in a wheel chair with legs made useless by polio.

Poor Ardis! What a day to be helpless in a wheel chair! Illi turned into the narrow road that wound back to the Enwright house, and took a deep breath of the crisp air that was full of the odor of damp leaves from the woods on her right. On her left were fields, still green with grass, all neatly enclosed with stretches of white rail fence. They belonged to Major Jim Wallace whose horses were pastured there. Just beyond the fence that bordered the road was a smaller fenced field with the jumps set up. Here his fine jumpers were schooled. This was the spot where Illi liked to linger when the horses were out. She would stand, one foot on the rail, watching the sleek brown or gray or black bodies stretch and arch themselves in the most beautiful curves in the world. Was there anything more beautiful than a horse in action? Was there a better friend anywhere than a horse?

But today the horses were mere dots in far pastures. There was no eager nose at the fence waiting for the sugar lumps which she slipped into her pocket in the school cafeteria. They were often at the fence as if they knew the bus schedule. Perhaps they did. Horses are smart, smarter than humans sometimes.

She rattled the sugar lumps in her pocket and went on up the stony road that led back to the farms off the highway. She didn't mind the stones. She'd walked barefoot on far worse roads than this. In fact she enjoyed this trip on foot from the bus. It was the only part of the day when she could be alone, when she could be herself without worrying about what other people were thinking of her, expecting of her. She wondered if she would ever again get used to having her life managed by other people.

For such a long time no one had cared about her comings and goings. She'd been on her own since she was ten, when Grandfather Laszlos had been taken away by the soldiers. She had had to think for herself then and only for herself. Imagine a little ten-year-old American girl doing some of the things she had had to do just to keep alive! There were some things she was ashamed of. She had had to learn to steal and lie and deceive. If she hadn't, she wouldn't be here now. She might not even have lived to reach the Children's Camp from which she had been chosen for the quota of refugee children to be sent to America.

Over there everyone had wanted to get to America, the land of the free, the land of plenty, where everyone was rich. It was said that in America people threw good food away, even potato parings and turnip tops, which everyone knows make good soup. She'd seen the garbage pails at the American officers' homes, she'd even pilfered from them. In America it was said there was enough for everyone, not for just the rich. She hadn't quite believed the story that the streets were paved with gold but she had been disappointed at the first sight of them when she'd landed from the boat. The cities were not beautiful like her beloved Budapest before the Nazis and the Russians came. Seen from the train, they had

7

seemed ugly and dirty and crowded just like the cities of Europe, except that there were no empty spots where the bombs had struck. She hadn't thought much of the cluttered back yards and the lines of wash hanging high between the tenement houses.

Yet there were lots of fine things in America, as she'd found out in the last few months: books and education and concerts and museums, all free to everybody, free radio and television programs, trains and buses that went places *on time*, houses big enough for everyone to have a room of his own like the comfortable Enwright home into which she had been so warmly received. In America even the working people had bathrooms and automobiles. And one couldn't tell whether a girl at school was rich or poor from the way she dressed. There were ice-cream sodas any day in the week and quarts of good fresh milk and an egg for breakfast and nylon stockings —and beautiful well-fed horses almost as fine as the ones at her grandfather's place in Kisber. Yes, America was a wonderful place. The terrible thing was that the boys and girls she had met did not appreciate it.

She sighed and rounded a bend in the road. Now that the trees were thinning she could see the Enwright house in the distance, white-plastered, green-shuttered, with a shingle roof so mossy it looked green, too. The house was set against a hillside so that it was a mixture of queer, unexpected levels. She could walk right from her bedroom out onto the hillside in back. It was a beautiful home, hers, as Mrs. Enwright kept telling her, but it was hard to believe that it belonged to her—or she to it. She was only beginning to accept her good luck, because at first she had been so terribly disappointed.

She had come there expecting to be a "daughter" in the house. The Enwrights had asked for a girl in her teens, one who would fit into their home, a quiet, refined, polite girl. Illi was all of these things. In Budapest, Hungary, her family had been of the well-thought-of professional class, her father a lawyer, her mother an artist whose portraits were exhibited at the best galleries. She knew her mother's grandfather had had a title, that there was an old castle somewhere in Austria where some cousins still lived. Maybe it was this knowledge that made her so proud, but it had also kept her from becoming low and beggarly, as were some of the homeless children she had met in her wanderings during and after the war. Always she had tried to keep her self-respect, her body clean, her clothes neat, her head high, never begging but taking what she had to as her right.

But when she came to the Enwrights she found a girl in a wheel chair for whom she was to be a companion. This had hurt because she thought she'd been brought here to wait on the girl. At home, companions had been paid help only a shade better than the other servants. She was to be a servant in this house, not a *daughter*. It had taken her weeks to realize that this was not so.

Again in America she found things so different. There was no real serving class as there had been at home, bowing and scraping and calling her father Excellency. Even Mrs. Grimm, the housekeeper at the Enwrights', whom nobody would have thought of calling by her first name, had a life of her own after her day's work. She went home at night to her own family and would have scorned the idea of being called a servant. She owned property

9

and her vote was as good as Mrs. Enwright's. Illi knew that Tom Grimm, her son, now in the Army, had been a welcome visitor at the Enwright house. Ardis was enthusiastic about him, his good nature, his ability on the baseball field. His dream was to become a big league player and Ardis was sure he would. It was "Tom this" and "Tom that" and Illi knew she wrote him long letters. No, all this could not have happened with the cook's son at home.

Maybe this was democracy, and at first she found it hard to accept. But thinking of it had gradually changed her ideas. She began to realize nobody considered her a servant or a poor dependent and that in her own way she would be able to do more for the Enwrights than they were doing for her. It restored her pride and gave her the feeling that she did belong in that pleasant white house waiting for her up the road.

Suddenly the day, the air, the warm sunshine, filled her with a sense of well-being. And, as if a spring had been released inside her, she began to run like a little girl, swinging her new leather book bag like one of the Indian clubs they'd had at the Children's Camp in Germany. The matron there, who'd once been a physical education teacher, had been enthusiastic about exercise, but Illi had not liked it. She had always been tired then. But now she felt so different. Three months of good food had done wonders for her thin frame, filled out the oval of her face, brightened her fair hair, and rounded her body until it filled her sweater properly.

She found herself gasping for breath and she dropped down on a big stone to rest. *"Ach, ich bin zu fett,"* she said half-aloud in the German in which she still thought

at times. "Oh, dear, I'm too fat. It is not fashionable to be fat in America."

And then she knew she was not alone. The knowledge brought the color flooding to her cheeks. For beyond the white fence a horse and rider had stopped and were both looking at her curiously. The horse was familiar, a roan which Major Wallace often rode, but the man or boy who rode him now was a stranger. He wore faded and much-cleaned cords with leather patches on the knees and a green pull-over sweater. His face was tanned a deep brown and his hair, faded from the sun, had red lights in it. His hazel eyes were deep-sunk with little squint wrinkles at the corners that made him look as if he were laughing. Maybe he was. But he sounded serious as he said, "I don't think you're too fat. Just pleasantly plump."

Illi jumped to her feet, her cheeks really flaming. "I —I do not often talk to myself," she stammered. "I—I am not that—that *närrisch*," she said, meaning stupid.

"Närrisch?" The boy laughed. "I'm not sure I know that word." He repeated it, his eyes regarding her more closely. "Say, you're new around here, aren't you?"

Illi nodded uncomfortably. "I live up the road," she said and picked up her bag to move on. "If you will excuse me I must hurry. Somebody is waiting for me up there."

"Oh, a date?" the boy said with a comical twist of his eyebrows.

But Illi did not answer. She walked away, her head up, listening for the soft pad of the horse's hoofs on the turf behind her. But it was quiet. She felt he must still be standing there looking after her. She wanted to turn and peep, but she kept on, her eyes on the road. Her head was so full of mixed thoughts she scarcely heard the station taxi coming toward her and had to move quickly out of its way. She wondered if it had come from the Enwright place, and whom it had brought there.

Chapter 2

*I*T WASN'T UNTIL she came to the broad gate across the Enwright lane that she dared to look back, but the horse and rider were off across the pasture in an easy, graceful canter. She stood watching until they disappeared from view. She wondered who the boy was. She knew that Major Wallace, whom she'd met several times at the Enwrights', was a widower with no children of his own; but the horse had been a Wallace horse and the boy had acted as if he belonged. Maybe he was just visiting, a nephew or something. Maybe Ardis would know.

There was something about the way he handled his horse that made her want to know him. He had good hands, gentle on the reins but keeping the horse under control. It was funny how much you could tell about people just by the way they treated horses, and the way horses treated them. This boy was a friend of horses, she could tell that. He rode just as Janni used to ride, careless but sure, as if the horse were part of his own easy-going body. For a moment her eyes blurred thinking of her brother with the dark, laughing eyes, "gypsy eyes" she used to call them to tease him. Where was Janni now?

Thinking of him and the horses brought back pictures of the old days at Kisber in the country in Hungary. It was like turning back the pages of a nursery book, not real any more but as familiar as her own name.

It had been weather like this that fall of 1943 before the Nazis came. She hadn't known why Janni and she had been sent away from Budapest to stay with Grandfather Laszlos in the country. She loved the huge, government-owned farm run by her grandfather for the breeding of horses, hundreds and hundreds of them. She had spent many vacations there and there had been a horse just for her, an exquisite little thoroughbred whom she had called Vidám.

Vidám was a yearling colt when he had been given to her and she had been the first to ride him, bareback at first and with a saddle later. Old Geza, the one-eyed groom who had once been a cavalryman under her grandfather, had taught her to ride correctly. She and Vidám had grown up together. He was a beautiful horse, the fine Arab strain showing in every motion, a gold chestnut color with a white star on his forehead and dainty white feet. His face was dished and his ears deli-

15

cate, but his chest was deep and his haunches strong. He had large, quick, bright eyes that seemed to know and understand every word she said, and he had a way of tossing his overly long forelock back as would a little girl whose hair gets in her eyes.

She turned away from watching the empty pasture and caught herself sighing deeply. She must not sigh for those lost days. She had promised herself not to. That time was over, it would never come again. She was seventeen now and beginning a new life, a very different life, as strange as—well, as one of those stories about space ships and trips to the moon that all the American girls and boys seemed to be reading, and perhaps believing, too. Only this life was very real. But like a trip to the moon, she couldn't turn back from it now even if she wanted to. She must make the best of it and be thankful.

She ran down the lane that dipped to a small plank bridge over the brook and mounted again to come to a stop beside the house that was set against the hill. There was a side door here and it led through a short hall directly to Ardis' room which was on the same level with the dining-living room and Mr. Enwright's study. Downstairs was the kitchen with its great stone fireplace, and upstairs were two bedrooms, hers and Mr. and Mrs. Enwright's.

The house had been chosen very carefully a year before when the Enwrights had bought it. They wanted a place where Ardis could wheel her chair freely in and out of doors and from room to room. Ardis had been a girl who loved the outdoors, and they knew the worst part of her illness would be her confinement within the four walls of one room. Here at least she could enjoy the sun and fresh air, the birds and the changing seasons, even if she could not go too far away.

"I think I have the nicest parents in the world," Ardis had told Illi the very first day she came. "They moved out here to the country just for me. I couldn't bear the idea of going away to a hospital or sanitarium, and they knew how I hated that old city apartment after—after I got sick. Even with the elevator it was a job to get out and to be pushed through the city streets with everyone looking at me in such a pitying way—ugh!" She shuddered. "I hated that part most of all. Here I can push myself anywhere I want to go, and there's so much to do and see."

Illi had soon found out that wherever Ardis was, there would always be a lot to do and to see. Life had not stopped for her just because part of her body seemed to have died.

"How—how long—" she had started to ask, and stopped. Maybe Ardis would never get well enough to walk.

"Oh, the doctor says I'll improve, very slowly of course. I go to the veterans' hospital near here—Daddy was in the war you know—for treatments. During the summer when it was hot enough I was lifted into the shallow pool that Daddy had built just for me. He and old Mr. Long, the carpenter, rigged up an apparatus to hold me up." She started to giggle. "You ought to see me. I sort of fly through the air with the greatest of ease like Peter Pan. I love it here. I have a good time but it's been hard on Dad and Mother. That's why I'm so glad you've come to live with us. It will relieve them. They are always so afraid I'll be lonesome."

Perhaps it was this one thing that showed Illi that in spite of its comforts and luxuries there were hard things to be borne in this land of plenty, too. Mr. and Mrs. Enwright had had to make a real sacrifice when they moved out here from the city. They were busy people with jobs that demanded long and unusual hours. Ardis had explained that her mother had given up her job with an advertising agency when polio had struck, but that with doctors' bills and nurses and hospitals it had been necessary for her to go back. Now her parents had to get up early to catch the seven fifty-three train for town, or else drive the forty miles into the city every day. It meant a late dinner, or no dinner at home at all. The girls seldom waited but ate alone, often at a small table on a smooth-paved terrace outside Ardis' room.

There was a cutting garden just beyond the side door and Illi stopped to pick a few of the last marigolds. Then she went into the house which seemed dark because the sun was still in her eyes. It was a lovely house inside, not grand, not *elegant* in the manner of rich Europeans with country estates, but it was *gemütlich*—such a hard word to explain in English. The nearest she could come to it was homelike. The house reflected the colorful, good taste of Mrs. Enwright who was an artist—not an artist like Illi's mother, but a commercial artist, as they called it here.

Illi threw her book bag on the top of an old chest that had been decorated in the Pennsylvania Dutch manner, much like the peasant pieces she had seen in the farmhouses in Hungary. She stopped for a moment at the door of Mr. Enwright's study. The room always fascinated her because it was literally lined with books from floor to ceiling. Books spilled off chairs and tables and were stacked in the corners. It was a terrible room to clean and Mrs. Grimm was always grumbling about it.

"What could anyone want with all these books?" Illi heard her say once to Mrs. Enwright. "He can't read them all."

"But he does read them, Mrs. Grimm," Mrs. Enwright had said.

"All of them?" Mrs. Grimm sounded doubtful.

"Most of them. That's his business. He has to tell people what to read so he has to read them himself first. But of course he knows how to skim, especially if the book isn't very good. It doesn't take him long to make up his mind."

Illi had meant to ask Mr. Enwright someday how he "skimmed" a book. Was it like skimming cream? But though he was a kindly man with a quick smile that lit up his round face with the shiny glasses that hid his dark eyes, he was not easy to talk to. He seemed to be "out of this world"—an expression she had just picked up in school. Illi knew he was book editor on a city paper and that when he wasn't reading books he was writing about them. And even in his spare time he couldn't get away from books because his hobby was collecting old ones, "first editions" he called them. Many of them were old and yellow and torn, and nobody, not Mrs. Grimm nor Mrs. Enwright, was allowed to touch them on their special shelves. When the dust got too much for Mrs. Grimm she would blow it away. Once Illi caught her at it and she had said, "Don't you dare tell on me, Illi. A little fresh air won't hurt these books any more than it hurts Ardis."

Illi spent a lot of time in this room when Mr. Enwright was not home, examining the books on the
shelves, her hands behind her back so she wouldn't be
tempted to touch them. The place smelled of tobacco
and old leather like her father's room in the house in
Budapest. It had had long windows opening out onto
her mother's garden where pebbled walks wound among
the flowers. Her father had a lot of books, too, and it
was there that Janni and she would amuse themselves
on rainy afternoons. There was one big book full of pictures, horrible but fascinating, of hell and demons, and
that was a favorite. It was so far removed from their
happy, carefree life that it never frightened them. They
didn't know then that some things were to happen to
their native land that would be just as horrible and ter-
rifying. She must ask Mr. Enwright some day if he had
that book among his treasures. She wondered how he
could find anything in this confusion. The place should
be catalogued like a library, she was thinking.

"I could do it if he would let me," she thought and
shrugged it off. "But he does not like strange fingers
handling his books. He must love them as I love horses."

The word horses brought up something else. She must
look up the English for *närrisch*. She must not be caught
using a foreign word again. Not that she was ashamed of
the German that had become her second tongue after
her native Hungarian, but she was determined to speak
as perfect English as she could.

Her hand was on the German dictionary when she
thought she heard voices in Ardis' room, one a girl's and
another deeper one, a man's. She shut the book and went
slowly down the hall, still holding the marigolds. Maybe

it was Tom Grimm, home on leave from camp, and if so she would now have a chance to meet him. But the pile of fine luggage outside in the hall was certainly not Tom's. She hesitated. Maybe she should go directly to her room. She had work to do there, something that was going to take time.

Then she changed her mind. She would just tell Ardis she was home. She didn't have to stay. She tapped lightly on Ardis' half-open door.

"Ardis, may I come in?" she called politely. She could never quite get used to the American habit of barging into a room without knocking.

"Illi? Come in, of course. I want you to meet someone. I've had the most wonderful surprise."

Illi pushed the door wide and stood there, her eyes roving over the big, bright room with windows like doors, chintz-covered bed and draperies, books, records, plants, and goldfish, and the girl in the wheel chair, her brown hair glowing like old walnut in the sun that slanted through a west window. Ardis was like her father, with a small round face and a cute upturned nose and freckles under her bright, round brown eyes. She was looking up with an expression almost of adoration at a tall young man who seemed to be enjoying her very evident admiration.

At sight of him Illi almost jumped with surprise and a little stab of fear. It was because he looked so much like the prosperous young Europeans that she had left behind her, the ones who had managed somehow to survive the war and hold on to their possessions. Many of them had been collaborationists, favorable to the enemy, but they weren't telling that now. They were the ones

21

whom the "lost" ones like herself despised heartily. What was he doing here?

This boy's hair was dark and slicked down to a fine polish. He wore it long, so different from the crew cuts she had seen on most American boys. He wore good tweeds cut in the skimpy English manner. A trench coat and a dark beret were thrown carelessly on a chair. She felt sure he would speak German or French or at least broken English. Then looking directly at him she caught the amused, mischievous glint in his dark eyes that was more like an American boy's way of looking at a girl. Who was he?

Ardis put out a brown hand to draw Illi closer. "Illi, this is my cousin, Mark Williams. Remember, the one I've told you about, who was always like a brother to me?"

Illi nodded but she could find no word to say. She just stared and the boy stared back, the look in his eyes deepening. Illi looked away. Then she knew what bothered her most. He had eyes like Janni, "gypsy eyes," laughing eyes.

"Mark's just back from Germany," Ardis was saying. "His father has been stationed over there for four years now. But Mark is home to stay. This is Illi, Mark, Ilona Horvath, whom I've been telling you about. You two should have lots to talk about. Mark's going to live with us, isn't that wonderful, Illi?"

She could hear Ardis' voice as if far off, explaining that Mark had come back to finish his studies at an American university, and her face stiffened into the mask she had worn for so long after she first came. So he was going to stay, live here, was he? He would be

22

taking her place. Ardis would have no further need for her. It would be Mark now. Mark would be her daily paper. Mark would push her chair out to the terrace, Mark would put her records on her player.

She hated him for all this as well as for his arrogance and those laughing eyes that looked like Janni's. He would probably look down on her. A refugee. He'd class her with the riffraff of Europe to which so many had sunk through starvation, suffering, and lack of homes. All her old resentment came back to her and with it the old pride.

Drawing herself to her full height, she threw back her head and tilted her chin as her mother used to do when she greeted people she didn't like. She would raise her hand, palm down . . . Suddenly she caught a glimpse of herself in Ardis' mirror, and for a moment she stared at herself in surprise. She looked so like her mother, blonde, tall, eyes blue as old china, but so cold and so proud. She dropped her hand limply. This was America. She was no great lady, only an American girl meeting an American boy.

"*Ich heisse Sie willkommen, Herr Williams,*" she said politely, "I welcome you, Mr. Williams," and to Ardis, "I am sure you are so happy to have your cousin here."

Mark raised his brows in surprise at her greeting, then bringing his heels sharply together he made her a bow as stiff and formal as any she had seen in her mother's drawing room. "*Ich freue mich, Ihre Bekahntschaft zu machen, Fräulein Horvath,*" he said. "I am so happy to meet you."

Ardis let out a hoot of amusement. "Oh, Mark, you

clown! You both sound like two people in a play. Don't pay any attention to Mark, Illi. He's just putting on an act. It's the best thing he does. Sit down, Illi, and tell us the news of the day."

But Illi shook her head. "You have company so I should like to be excused. I have an important thing to do in my room."

Head up she turned, still clutching the flowers, and left the room—but not too quickly to hear Mark say, "Wow! Such *Formalität!* If the flowers in her lily-white hand had been a gun, she'd have shot me down. You didn't tell me, Ardis, that you had gone to the nobility for a companion."

With a cry that was half a sob, half a snort, Illi dropped the flowers in the wastebasket as she went by, and mounted the steps to her own room.

Chapter 3

*T*HE BOXED-IN STAIRS to Illi's room were steep and crooked, winding around the big chimney, quaint and in keeping with the old house that had once been the home of simple people, but no stairs for a grand exit. Yet with Mark's words in her ears, Illi took them proudly, body straight as an arrow, her head still lifted high.

Sunshine flooded the upper hall from the open door of her room, but when she entered she closed the door and locked it for the first time in months and stood against it as if trying to shut something out. She felt the same as she'd felt in those first weeks at the Enwrights'. Then her room had been an escape. She'd felt she was locking out a too-curious world. Now she wanted to lock out the picture of Ardis downstairs laughing with Mark over things she knew nothing about, maybe even over her.

"I'm just jealous," she told herself, trying to be reasonable, but she knew it was more than jealousy. Fear was there, fear that Mark had come back to replace her and that they wouldn't need her any more. They might even send her away. They could. They had not adopted her, only promised to take care of her until she could take care of herself. And she could do that now that her English was so much better.

But, she told herself, surely the Enwrights would not do a thing like that. They were kind people, both of them, but still if they didn't like her . . . She had known at first that they didn't. She could tell. She remembered the expression on Mrs. Enwright's face the first time she had seen her. It was just a passing expression, lasting only a moment, but Illi had caught it and thought, "She does not like me, I know."

She went to her mirror now to look at the girl who was so different from the girl who had landed with the other DP children in June. She could hardly blame Mrs. Enwright, who had come with the agency lady to meet her.

"I must have looked like a scarecrow," she said half aloud, running the comb through hair that was now bright and lively and cut so that its natural curl showed up in soft waves and upturned ends. Then it had been long and uncared for, dull and stringy, and she had worn it caught back with two little gray combs that an old lady on the boat had given her. Everything she had had on was a hand-me-down, her skirt so large she had to take a big tuck in the waistband, her sweater stretched and baggy. She had been wearing cotton stockings and shoes with paper in the toes because they were too long. She had been skinny and she had had that gray look that comes from bad feeding. Her eyes were dark, sunken coals over her high cheekbones.

"I am not what she expected," she had told herself then, and it had made her awkward and tongue-tied, unable to use even the little English she had learned. Her face had been frozen so that she couldn't smile when Mrs. Enwright smiled at her. It had been a bad beginning and Illi had not done much to help things. She had not tried to make people like her. That hard shell which for years she had grown around herself, as a protection against the people she feared or suspected, had taken a long time to crack. It was Ardis who had done it.

It had happened on a rainy day in June. They'd been sitting in Ardis' room listening to the rain on the roof that was making harmony with the music on the radio. Ardis was doing crossword puzzles. She loved them and she had insisted that Illi should help her, "because it will do so much for your English," she had said. Illi had tried but it was not easy.

"Here's a six-letter word for an East Indian sailor, beginning with LA and ending with R," Ardis said suddenly. "Would you mind looking it up in Dad's big dictionary, Illi?"

Illi had gone to Mr. Enwright's study to leaf through the big book on its stand. She had just found the word, *lascar*, when the music in the other room stopped abruptly. She hurried back to see if anything was the matter. But Ardis was just closing the lid of the record player beside her chair and her eyes were shining with mischief.

"Is anything wrong?" Illi asked anxiously.

"No, of course not. Sit down, Illi, and listen. I have a surprise for you."

Illi sat down on the big puffy ottoman beside Ardis' chair, wondering why Ardis was so mysterious. Then the music came and her eyes opened wide in astonishment. It was *Itt Hagyon a Falutokat*, an old Hungarian folk song, and it was sung by Erno Karolyi. Illi heard it through without a word, but inside she felt her heart was breaking.

"Wait, there are more," Ardis said excitedly. "Here are two of Zoltán Kodály's records and one of Béla Bartók's, all folk songs, so Daddy said. He looked all over the record shops until he could find them for you." She changed the record quickly.

Illi leaned back and shut her eyes. *Akkor Szep az Erdö:* The forest is beautiful; *Kit Kéne Elvenni?:* Whom ought one to marry?; and *Cigánynóta*, the Gypsy Song. The lovely, plaintive music brought it all back. How often she had heard old songs like these played on the *tilenko*, the shepherd's pipe, out on the *puszta*, the prairielike pastures where they tended their sheep. So much of Hungarian music was mournful, but it was fresh and clear like the winy air of the *puszta* itself. She listened as one melody followed another, some sung, some played on the violin. They brought back so much: her mother's voice singing as she worked in her little studio across the pebbled garden, the young grooms

28

at night in their quarters beyond the stables at Kisber, the excitement of a czardas danced at a country fair or a village wedding or a gypsy camp. She could feel the tears start behind her eyes and she tried to wink them back, but two big ones got away and ran down her cheeks. Then she had felt Ardis' hand on hers.

"Let them come, Illi," Ardis said softly. "It's all right. You'll feel better now. It's such beautiful music. But I can't understand the words. You must tell me what they mean."

Illi put on the first record again, *Itt Hagyon a Faluto-kat*, and as the music filled the room she translated it slowly into English:

"Now I leave my little village,
   Soon I will leave for a foreign country
   Far, far away.
   In the dark of the night with no stars in the sky
   I will say good-by
   So nobody will see my tears.
   When I leave, don't talk about me
   Because I never wanted to hurt anyone.
   You cannot reproach me,
   I have made no mistakes except the one
   That I loved you, beloved."

"It sounds like a lover's good-by," Ardis said. "How sad but how lovely!"

"Yes," Illi said. "There is a sadness about Hungarian music. There is also a gladness. It is said, you know, that we Hungarians . . ."

"*We* Hungarians?" Ardis had teased.

"Well, I am not an American yet. I must be something."

"Of course, I was only teasing, Illi. Go on, tell me about the Hungarians."

"I was about to say that we Hungarians say of ourselves that we cry with one eye and laugh with the other. I think it explains us very well."

"Indeed it does. It explains you, Illi. But tell me more."

So she had told Ardis, and in the telling she could feel the shell inside her breaking up under the warmth of the kindness about her, just as the ice breaks in the spring under the warmth of the sun. She had told Ardis about the garden in Budapest and her mother's little studio not much bigger than a doll's house, about Janni, her brother with the laughing eyes, about Grandfather Laszlos and his big mustache, and about Geza, the old groom, and Vidám, the most beautiful horse that ever lived.

"And I wasn't even going to think of them any more," she'd said, blowing her nose.

"But you must. Don't try to forget them, Illi. They are a part of you even if they are gone. Lots of things in my life are gone too, and may never happen again. But I like to think about them, things like skating on a winter afternoon at the Rockefeller Plaza rink in New York, like whacking a ball down the hockey field." She had smoothed out her blanket thoughtfully over her useless knees. "But there will be other things to take their place. Do you know, Illi, you and I are rather alike. We've got to build up new lives for ourselves. Maybe it will help if we do it together."

After that it was different. She began to feel that there

was a reason for her being in this house. Even Mrs. Enwright must have noticed it because one day she said, "Illi, what are you going to call me? I can't be Mrs. Enwright forever. You belong to us, you know, you're a part of the family."

Illi had been caught off guard. She could feel the ice closing over again. "What would it please you to be called, Mrs. Enwright?" she asked politely.

Mrs. Enwright had laughed in her easy way. "It isn't what I want, it's what you feel like calling me. I'm different things to different people, Mary to my mother, Petey to my husband, Aunt Mims to my favorite nephew, and Polly to my old school friends. And of course to Ardis I am Mother—the best name of all," she added wistfully and seemed to be waiting for Illi to say it.

But Illi couldn't. She had just shaken her head and murmured, "I do not know yet."

"Well, take your time. It will come to you. I can wait," Mrs. Enwright said so kindly that it made Illi feel small and uncomfortable.

That night lying in bed she had tried out a lot of names, and by the time Mrs. Enwright had stopped at her door to say good night, she had decided.

"Good night, *Mütterchen*," she had whispered.

"*Mütterchen!* Little mother! I like that." Mrs. Enwright had come into her room and leaned down to kiss her warmly. "That's my girl," she said softly. "I knew things would work out all right."

But now with Mark here they wouldn't. Oh, why did he have to come back just now when she had begun to feel sure of herself?

31

She turned from the glass to look at the little room she had come to love. Even *it* looked different now that there seemed a chance she might lose it. It was such a pretty room and it had been waiting for her when she came; all green and yellow, yellow paint with ivied paper that went up the walls and over the ceiling, too. There was a yellow homespun chair and ruffled curtains to match the yellow organdy skirt of a dressing table set into a dormer window.

Mrs. Enwright had thought of everything. There were shelves for books and ornaments under the sloping ceiling, a small bedside radio, and a sewing machine in the closet, because on Illi's list of qualifications it had said she could sew. She had learned that from a poor German seamstress who had taken her in for a few months. Frau Werner could turn sheets and tablecloths and draperies into the most wonderful clothes. During that winter Illi had made a warm coat which she had designed herself and cut from an old blanket. She had worn it to shreds.

That was the winter when she began to sketch in earnest with a stump of a pencil, using anything she could find. She had always loved to draw but she had never had any instruction, and her fingers itched to work out the designs that danced in her head. Even now her schoolbooks were full of doodling that was far more than meaningless lines. Miss Patchin, the home ec. teacher, said Illi showed great originality and a feeling for color and texture and that she should plan to study costume design when she finished high school.

She went over and opened the door that led directly onto the hillside. She loved this little private entrance of hers, and often at night she would go outside in her bare feet and pajamas to look up at the sky and say her prayers of thanks that God had brought her to such a good home at last. But now if Mark stayed, it might not be hers for long. Where would he sleep? There was no other bedroom. Would they move her out and move Mark in?

Then she thought she heard voices on the other side of the house and she ran up the hill where she could see the driveway and barn, which was now only a garage and tool house. Two people were walking toward it: Mark, laden with his two heavy bags, a tennis racket, and a guncase, and after him Mrs. Grimm, burdened with broom, mop, and pail. Then Illi remembered. There was a room of sorts, a feed room in the upper barn, which the Enwrights had talked of making into a place for guests. So this was to be Mark's quarters. She laughed softly, wondering how he would like its crudeness, the mice and the pigeons, the chipmunks rattling their nuts over his head on the shingled roof. She'd heard them when she had stolen over there to be by herself.

Illi had no fear of barns, empty or filled with cattle. They were friendly places to her. She had slept in so many of them, deep under the hay to keep warm and sometimes to hide from unfriendly troopers. If Mark didn't like his barn quarters she would take them. She wouldn't mind that too much.

She went back to her room feeling better now that this difficulty seemed solved, and unlocked her door, opening it wide so she could hear the bell that Ardis kept by her side. Tinkerbell they called it, after Peter Pan's fairy. She listened closely before she went to her desk and pulled out a large pad of paper. She had a big and important job to do—her own story. It was for Miss Loudon who taught Junior English.

"For your theme this week I want you all to write 'The Story of My Life,'" Miss Loudon had said with her crooked little laugh. "I think I ought to get some interesting papers out of that topic."

Writing English was getting easier for Illi every day. There were not nearly so many little red marks on her papers, *sp*, *punc*, *gram*, and *vocab*, as there had been. But it was going to be hard to talk about herself. She hoped Miss Loudon would not decide to read it in class as she sometimes did. The class would not believe it. They would think she was putting it on pretty thick. Still it had to be done.

She wrote the title in her neat, pointed handwriting and began:

I was born in Budapest on April 26, 1936, Shakespeare's birthday, as my father used to tell me. It made me feel very

34

proud to share a birthday with such a great man. In those days Budapest was a very beautiful city. I have not seen it since the bombings. I do not think I should want to.

Budapest is really two cities, Buda on the right bank of the Danube, Pest on the left. They are connected by six bridges. Buda is built on the hills. It was a beautiful sight at night to look up there from the Danube Embankment and see the great lights thrown on the Observation Tower and the Coronation Church where the crown of St. Stephen, the patron saint of Hungary, lies. My father often took me there on Sunday afternoons and we would look far down to see the streetcars crawling along and all the little crooked

streets climbing up the hills. There were four stone lions there, two friendly looking, and two very fierce. I called them Matthew, Mark, Luke, and John.

There was another spot my mother and father used to take me to, a place called Margareten Island, between the two cities with beautiful gardens and grass like green velvet.

That is where the nightingales sang. Have you ever heard a nightingale? It is lovely music, sweeter even than a canary.

Illi stopped and gazed out the window to where the crows were making a racket in the big sycamore. So different from the nightingale's song! This was like writing about a dream, a lovely dream from which she hated to wake up. She could see herself in the dream, a little girl with bright golden hair and blue, blue eyes, dressed in a red coat and holding tight to her brother Janni's hand while they watched the pigeons rise and dip behind the Racoksi Monument in front of the Parliament buildings. She bent to her job:

I had a very happy childhood. My parents were not rich but we seemed to have everything we needed, and lived in a large house, a cook in the kitchen, and a parlor maid, too. They came from my mother's country, close to Austria, and were fat and jolly and talked with high, giggly voices. My brother, Janni, who was five years older than I, took a lot of care of me. He was fun and good to me. My mother was usually busy painting in her studio, which was a little house at the foot of our garden. We had a lot of company, people who did interesting things like my mother and my father who was a lawyer. They had wonderful times until things began to change. Then their faces grew sober and they would sit talking in whispers in the dark.

Then it all ended. One day my mother came into the study where Janni and I were playing with his soldiers and our father's books. Her face was white and scared, but she said in a way that did not frighten us, "How would you like to go to Grandfather Laszlos for Christmas?" We cried with joy. We had never been there in the winter and we were full of plans for sledding and skating and skiing. But one thing was wrong. Our parents were not going with us. "We shall be too busy here," my mother said.

Kati, a young Hungarian maid, was to go with us and it seemed our mother packed a great deal for such a short vacation. We were surrounded with boxes and bags and cases when she and our father kissed us good-by in the compartment of the train. There were tears rolling down their faces and ours. That was the last time I saw them. They were imprisoned and killed, as were a lot of other patriotic Hungarians who did not want to see their country invaded first by the Germans and then by the Russians. Poor Hungary!

But I did not know all this then. At the station we were met as usual by the big coach with the four black horses

driven by a coachman with a ribboned whip. It took us out to the big breeding farm that my grandfather ran for the government with hundreds and hundreds of fine English thoroughbreds and Arabian horses on acres and acres of pastureland. We were to stay in the old castle where my grandfather had his quarters. It did not seem strange to be riding in a coach like Cinderella's to an old castle. There were lots of castles in Hungary. In the country there were still princes and peasants. In this castle was one suite that was always kept closed because it had been used once by the Empress Elizabeth. It was like Bluebeard's closet to me. Once when it was being cleaned I was able to peep inside and I saw the great canopied bed with the coat of arms woven in gold into the crimson damask. It was all very, very grand and elegant. Later on I saw it opened by the German soldiers who tracked mud and stable dirt all over the beautiful flowered carpets.

The Germans came in March, 1944. My grandfather was worried when he heard they were on their way to Kisber. He called Janni and me to him. "There is nothing we can do but make as little trouble as possible. I want you and Janni to keep out of their way, stay in your rooms with Kati." But by the time the German soldiers did come I was alone. Janni woke me up one night to say he was running off with some of the young grooms to join the guerrillas in the hills. That was the last time I saw Janni. The next day Kati ran away, too, to join her sweetheart in the village which "collaborated" with the Germans.

My grandfather continued to run the place for the Germans, who probably felt they did not know enough to do it themselves. But later they knew enough to get the horses away before the Russians came. We were all ordered to go, horses, grooms, and their families, on freight trains across the border to Germany. Of course Vidám went with us.

It was not so bad there at first, not until the war began to go against the Germans and there was not enough food for

the horses. Geza and I would manage to steal enough for
Vidám though. One day they caught me with my apron
full of fodder. What a fuss! I acted like a wild animal. I
screamed and kicked and bit the guard, and another guard
came running up with a whip. But my grandfather heard
it and came running too. He was a strong man and he got
the whip out of the guard's hands. But Grandfather knew it
was the end for him. "They will come for me, Illi," he said
when he had hurried me into the house. "I want you to go
to Mrs. Czerny, the wife of one of the grooms, and ask her
to hide you. I will say you have run away."

But I did not go to Mrs. Czerny. I was too scared by
those guards. I hid until my grandfather was taken away,

and in the dark I went out to say good-by to Vidám. I
wanted to take him with me but I knew it would make too
much noise and I would be caught. So I ran away alone.

The rest of this story I do not like to think about and so
I do not think I could write it very well. This was the end

of the real me anyway, the well-bred little girl, Ilona Horvath. After that I became someone else, one of the lost children of Europe who lived from day to day the best way they could and—

A soft tinkle brought Illi back to the present. She went to the hall to listen. It was Tinkerbell. She hurried down the stairs to Ardis' room.

"Can I do something for you?" she asked anxiously.

"No. I was just worried about you," Ardis said. "You've been sitting up there alone so long—you look funny, Illi. As if you'd been far away and had just come back."

Illi gave a short laugh. "I have been far away. I have been writing the story of my life," she said.

"All of it?"

"No, just the beginning, the nice part."

"But this is nice, too, isn't it, Illi?"

"Ye-es, it was until—"

"Until what?"

But Illi could not bring herself to ask about Mark. "Never mind," she said. "It is not so important."

Ardis shook her head. "You're a funny girl, Illi. Just when I'm beginning to think I know you well, you shut up again like a clam. Please, Illi, don't be like that!"

"I—I cannot seem to help it," Illi said and went to look out the window so Ardis would not see her tears. "It is so hard," she tried to explain, "especially when you do not know what the next chapter is going to be."

Chapter 4

IT WAS QUITE a gay dinner the night of Mark's arrival. Both Mr. and Mrs. Enwright hurried home to greet their nephew and to hear the news of his family whom he had left behind in Germany. His mother was Mrs. Enwright's sister who had married her West Point cadet after his graduation and had wandered around the world with him ever since. Mark had two younger sisters, still with their parents in Germany.

"They envied me getting back here to America," he told his aunt.

"Is it so bad over there now?" Mrs. Enwright asked.

"Oh no, Aunt Mims, not for Americans. We get all

the good food we need and there is plenty of help. There are always some poor down-and-outers who are only too glad to work in the officers' houses where they get good meals and the left-overs to take home. You know I've never had to shine my own shoes since I left home?"

"Well, I wouldn't brag about it," Ardis said quickly.

"You'll find it a very different story over here," Mr. Enwright said with a look at his wife.

The conversation was changed quickly, but not before it had brought back some unpleasant memories for Illi. She had been one of those who had worked in an American officer's home. It was something she had not told the Enwrights, not even Ardis, because she had not been happy about it at all. She had been sent from the Camp in response to a request from one of the officers' wives. She needed a responsible girl who could sew and who knew English, and Illi had been chosen.

At first she had been delighted because it seemed to offer a way out for her. The idea of getting to America had been uppermost in her mind for some time, ever since she had realized she could never go back to Hungary. She had been studying English, getting ready for just such an opportunity. So she had tried to make herself invaluable in the American household. But it had not worked out the way she hoped. Mrs. Lyons, the young captain's wife, was kind, gay, but used to being waited upon. Illi soon found herself doing all sorts of things, from playing lady's maid to baby-sitter. She even found herself acting as hostler on occasion because Mrs. Lyons liked to ride, and Illi would be sent to bring the horse from the stables a mile away. This part Illi did not mind because it gave her a chance to ride herself and she found the old skills that old Geza had taught her coming back to her. She was even able to pass on some of her knowledge of horsemanship to Mrs. Lyons, who in her turn would let Illi have the horse for a few hours on her day off.

She had stuck it out with the Lyons family for six months, but all that came of it was the renewal of her good riding habits, the use of English with a Georgia accent, and some hand-me-down clothes. When the Lyonses went back to America they didn't even try to take her. Illi had to go back to the Camp and hope she would be lucky enough to be included in the DP quota. But she had seen a lot in those months. She had found out how Americans lived and dressed. She had seen their easy manners, envied the carefree young people who came in the front door as she went out the back.

After dinner she asked to be excused and went back to her room to finish her English paper. And the next day when she came down to breakfast Mark was gone. He had driven into town with his aunt and uncle on business of his own.

When Illi dropped off the bus that afternoon she could not recapture the feeling of well-being that had filled her the day before. Her feet lagged as she went up the stony road. There would be nothing to come home to any more. Ardis would have Mark, and the cozy afternoons in Ardis' room would come to an end. Maybe she should try to get an afterschool job. There was to be one in the smartest dress shop in town, so Miss Patchin had told her. They needed a girl for two hours

43

every afternoon and all day on Saturdays. She wondered if she had better not look into it. It would make her less dependent upon the Enwrights, and if she weren't as necessary to them now she would at least be less expense.

She had come to the bend in the road and as she rounded the trees she was surprised to see the boy waiting at the rail fence. He was on the same horse, but today he wore jeans and an old leather jacket.

"Hi!" he said.

"Hi!" said Illi and kept on walking.

"Wait! I want to talk to you. You're the girl who lives with the Enwrights, aren't you?"

Illi nodded.

"I should have known that yesterday, but I had forgotten until I happened to mention you to the Major. He told me all about you."

"All? What did he tell you?" Illi asked, all the newly aroused bitterness coming to the tip of her tongue.

"Oh, nice things." The boy grinned in a friendly way. "What else could he say?"

"Plenty, and some not so nice. He could have said I was a poor war orphan whom the Enwrights took in out of pity and may now be sorry they did." She could feel the tears of self-pity pricking back of her eyes.

The boy slid off the horse and came over to the fence. "Oh, come now," he said in a worried way, "that isn't so, and you know it isn't. The Major thinks the Enwrights were very lucky to get you in the family as a sister for—Ardis, is that her name?"

Illi nodded again, wondering just how much he was stretching the truth.

"I bet you've just had a hard day," he went on. "We

44

all have them. I'm out working off a grouch myself. I flunked my German test yesterday. I can't seem to get the hang of that awful language."

"It is not awful," Illi said stoutly. "It is a beautiful language when you understand it."

"And you do, don't you?"

"Yes, as well as my own, better than English."

"What is your own language?"

"Hungarian. But I have not used it for years. I—I was living in Germany and Austria during the war and afterward."

"That must have been an experience," he said and swung himself over the fence. "I've always wanted to travel. I guess that's one reason I'm aiming for the Point."

"The Point?"

"Yes, West Point, where they train officers for the Army, you know."

"Oh yes, I have heard of it. So you want to be a fight-ing man and go to war?"

"Goodness no! Only, the way things look I may have to, and I'd like to do it in style."

"In style." Illi repeated and gave him a long, serious look. "There is no style in war. It is a horrible thing, for everyone. The German officers lived in style and rode in style in big cars—but where are they now?" She was thinking of the beautiful room in the castle at Kisber and the trampled carpet and torn draperies which had been high style before the German officers despoiled them or took them home to their wives, perhaps.

"Yes, where are they now? I often wonder about that," the boy said thoughtfully. He was looking off

45

across the rolling meadows to the faint line of blue hills, as if he wanted to see beyond them all the way to the other side of the world. "You see, my father was killed in the Battle of the Bulge."

"Oh, I'm sorry," Illi said as suddenly sympathetic as she had been bitter.

"Thanks, but I'm not looking for sympathy. That happened some time ago and I hardly remember him now. But I guess I gave you the wrong impression about my plans. You see, it's this way: my Dad was with the Major over there. He only got to be a top sergeant but the Major sort of relied on him. He felt pretty bad when my Dad was killed, and when he came home he looked up Mom and me and brought us here. Mom's his house-keeper and I'm supposed to help out with the horses after school."

"Do you like that?"

"School or the horses?"

"Both."

"Well, I'm crazy about horses and I like school better than I did. You see, I sort of fooled away my last year at High. I just made the grade but no more. It didn't worry me because I would think, 'What do I need with science and math and history just to take care of a stable of horses?' But this summer the Major got at me. He said I ought to get an appointment to West Point as the son of a veteran. But you have to pass a competitive exami-nation for that, with mental, medical, and physical apti-tude tests. It was the mental part that worried me. So he sent me over to the Waverly Academy for this year. He said it would make it easier for me when I take the exams for the Point, and if I didn't pass, the extra education wouldn't hurt me." He grinned at her like a naughty little boy.

"Of course it would not. Education never hurt anybody." She looked at him in a puzzled way. "But I don't believe your heart is in it, is it?"

"Well . . ." He looked off across the green pastures as if he could see into the years ahead. "I'm really an outdoor person, I guess, and I know if I got into the Army I'd like it. But being cooped up in a classroom gets me sometimes. But the Major is so set on this business that it's the least I can do for him."

"And for your father, too, perhaps?"

"Yes. I guess you hit the real reason. Anyway, here I am boning away instead of being out all day with the horses or out on the football field with the team. I was a pretty good quarterback last year."

"Oh, you must be the boy Geegee was talking about."

"Geegee Fairchild?"

"Yes. She thinks it is a shame for any boy who was such a good player as you were to pass it all up. She cannot understand you."

The boy laughed. "Gee couldn't, not with that little peanut brain of hers. She's fun, but nothing from here up." He made a motion across his neck with his hand.

"She has been very nice to me," Illi defended her friend.

"Why wouldn't she? You know something? I haven't told anyone but you why I'm doing what I'm doing. I mean about trying for the Point."

"And why have you told me?"

"I don't know. Do you?"

"Maybe because you know I will not tell. I will not,

47

you know. I have kept more secrets than this. I know how to keep my mouth shut."

"I bet you do. Say, I don't even know your name."

"Ilona Horvath—Illi, they call me."

"And mine's Neal Austin. Hi, Illi!" He smiled at her companionably.

"Hi, Neal!" She smiled back. She felt better now. How short a time it had taken to put her whole world to rights again!

They had been standing together, their backs against the fence, their arms on the rail, and now Illi suddenly felt something warm and soft press between them. It was a horse's curious nose.

Neal laughed. "It's Rockabye. I guess he wants to get into the act."

"He is jealous," Illi said, holding out her hands to the quivering nostrils. "My horse used to do that whenever I talked to someone else."

"Your horse? Have you a horse?"

"Not now. That was in the old days in Hungary. My grandfather raised horses for the Hungarian government, Arabians and English thoroughbreds. They were fine horses, very famous."

Neal seemed impressed. "We don't see many Arabians around here. But the Major has some fine thoroughbreds. He has a racing stable, you see, but he keeps a few good riding horses too, like this boy. He's only good for hacking. Has the nicest running walk, puts you to sleep if you don't look out. Doesn't it, Rockabye?"

The horse neighed delightedly and jerked up his head as if to say, "What are we doing standing here just talking?"

48

"Look," Neal said impulsively, "if you like horses you ought to see the Major's stables. Why don't you come over now? I'd like to show you around. Give you a ride, too, if you like."

"I would like that so much," Illi said. "But I would have to change." She looked down at her best gray flannel suit which she had put on that morning to impress Mark who wasn't there. Then she remembered Ardis. If Mark were not home Ardis would be alone.

"I tell you what I shall do," she said. "I shall go home, and if Ardis does not need me I shall change and come right over. But do not wait for me too long."

"I'll wait, don't worry," Neal said. "But don't be too long. I'd like you to see the place in daylight."

Illi went up the lane to the Enwright gate and now her steps were light and eager. The friendliness of the boy with the rough hair and the ready smile had pulled her out of her low spirits. And the prospect of seeing the Major's horses at close range was a pleasant thing to look forward to, provided, of course, Ardis was not alone.

But as she crossed the small bridge and climbed the lane to the yard she could see a strange car in the parking place. It was a small, foreign-looking car, the kind that one saw so much on the streets of Europe. It had had a new coat of tan paint but she could see the car wasn't new. The leather upholstery was worn and the chrome was dull. But it looked quite exciting in that quiet country setting. It meant that Ardis had company.

She tiptoed through the side door and down the hall to listen outside Ardis' door. To her surprise she heard Mark's voice saying, "She's a pip, Ardis. A motor like a pussy cat. Look, let me get your coat and I'll push your

49

pram outside so you can get a good look-see at her."

"But Mark, you said your father gave you only enough money for a little old jalopy, just something to get you to school and back every day."

"I know. But I couldn't resist this baby. So I used the money Dad gave me for a down payment. I can carry the rest for twenty-five dollars a month."

"But twenty-five dollars! Oh, Mark, you're such a crazy fool about cars. You always were. How are you going to get that much money out of your monthly allowance?"

"Don't worry, I'll get it somehow. The old American initiative isn't dead. I'll make that Jag earn its keep. Why, I can save it on gas. Come on, hurry up. I want you to take a look at my beauty."

"All right," she heard Ardis say. "I wonder where Illi is. I wish she were here to see it, too."

"Illi would probably stick her pretty little nose so high it would touch her eyebrows," Mark said. "Has that baby got airs! But they're all the same, those DPs. Too fine for their own good."

"Oh, Mark, don't talk that way, please." Ardis seemed really disturbed. "If you knew what Illi's been through . . ."

"I know. Don't forget I've been living over there with them for years."

"Then you ought to be more sympathetic. Illi's still scared, Mark. She doesn't trust anyone. That's what makes her seem so cold and offish. She isn't really, when you know her. Why I—I love Illi, Mark, and I do want you two to be friends."

"Oh, I'm willing to be friendly. If Fraülein Illi would

just forget that chip on her shoulder, she could be quite a knockout. Here's your coat—let's go!"

Illi tiptoed up the stairs to her own room. She did a lightning change into jeans and a pale blue sweater and tied a blue ribbon around her fair head. A knockout, was she? She wondered if Neal would think so. She left her room by the hill door and angled down the bank before Mark could wheel Ardis' chair around the corner of the house.

Chapter 5

ONE ENTRANCE TO the big Wallace place lay up the narrow road beyond the Enwright lane. Illi had passed it many times, but she had never had any reason to open the white gate and walk up the long tree-lined lane to the house set so far from the road it was not visible.

Although the Enwrights were on visiting terms with the Major, Illi had never been asked to visit there. Now she hoped that Neal would be waiting for her at the stables and that she wouldn't run into the Major. She was a little afraid of him. Maybe it was because he was a military man and she was afraid of all military men. To her they meant only trouble. The Major, the few times she had seen him, seemed kindly enough, but he was brusque and liked things done his way. She could understand why Neal felt he had to do what the Major wanted. She knew he was retired because of an injury, a bad knee that did not, however, keep him out of the saddle. Whenever he came over to the Enwrights' he rode over, jumping on a horse the way most people hop into a car.

She was standing in the road, trying to get up her courage, when she heard the soft clop of hoofs and looked up the lane to see Neal coming along on Rockabye and leading another horse, a stud colt not more than two years old and tacked up for riding. He was a perfect little chestnut with a white star on his forehead and dark, wide-set eyes, proudly arched neck, and four dainty white stockings.

Illi stood rooted to the spot. She must be dreaming, because it was exactly like the dream, the one that still came back to her, the one from which she always awoke with a feeling of keen disappointment. It was the dream where she saw Vidám coming down from the Kisber stables, headed straight for her. It was a little game that Geza had played with her. He would saddle Vidám, give him a gentle slap, and send him off to meet her. But Vidám would not budge until she called, *"Vidám, gyere ide*—Vidám, come here!" Then the colt would come running to Illi like one playmate to another, come to a dead stop, and toss back his forelock as if to say, "What do you want, little one?" Then she would mount and they would be off on their rambles. But in the dream she never got that far. She would wake up or the dream would change.

Now she watched fascinated as Neal dropped the reins and said, "Sugar, Pokey. Look who's waiting for you. Can't keep a nice girl like that waiting, can we, boy?" and gave him a gentle slap.

"*Gyere ide!*" she called out, and to her surprise the colt came running to her and stopped, giving his head an impatient toss.

"How do you like him?" Neal said, coming up on Rockabye and giving her the sugar he held in his hand.

"I—I love him," Illi said, still in a trance, and let the horse take the sugar from her fingers. "Who taught him to do that?"

"I did. He's a smart little cookie, understands everything you say. I thought we might ride up the road a bit before we go back to the stables. If you're afraid you can't manage him I'll swap. Sometimes Pokey is a bit frisky."

"I shall manage him all right, won't I, Pokey?" Illi said. "We are friends already, see?" The horse's ears pricked forward and he lowered his head sidewise as he gave a pleased short snort. It was almost like winking an eye. "What is his full name?" she asked, a critical eye on the bit. "That martingale, is it too tight?"

"No, it has to be tight. He carries too high a head. His real name is Hocus-pocus."

"What a queer name for a horse! You Americans always pick such funny names, no dignity in them."

"Perhaps there's no dignity in Pokey," Neal said with a short laugh. "Sometimes he's a regular little clown of a horse. You'll see. Shall I give you a hand up?"

"I should say not," Illi said scornfully and swung herself into the saddle like an old hand. She hadn't been on

54

a horse for several years now but it seemed just like yesterday. As they wound slowly down the road it still had the quality of her dream. In fact Pokey was uncannily like Vidám, except in coloring. Vidám had been lighter, a gold chestnut. There had been a lot of Arabian in Vidám, the dished face, the arched neck, the flowing mane, and the tail carried high and proudly like a plume.

"Where did the Major get this horse, Neal?" she asked.

"Oh, in some kind of a deal. He comes from a famous stud farm down in Maryland. It belongs to a friend of the Major's and he won't have an unregistered horse on the place. This little guy couldn't be registered."

"Why not? Isn't he a thoroughbred? He looks as if he were or at least a half-bred. Don't they know who his dam and sire were?"

Neal shrugged. "They should. He was born down there but it seems there are some good horses going around that they can't register because they have no papers, no proof of ownership. Like a house or a car without a clear title, I guess. The Jockey Club won't recognize their get as full thoroughbreds for racing. I think that accounts for Pokey. Too bad, because he has good blood in him. You can see that."

"So what becomes of him?" Illi asked thoughtfully.

"Oh, the Major will keep him and use him some other way. He may turn into a good hunter, or jumper. He can clear a good three-foot hurdle already in open field. I'll take him over the jumps and show you one of these days."

They rode on in silence for a few moments, then Illi

55

said dreamily, "My horse was named Vidám. It means happy-go-lucky, gay."

"Very nice," said Neal. "I've never heard that name before. You must have loved your little horse very much."

"I did," Illi said soulfully.

"What happened to him?"

"I do not know. I had to leave him behind me when I —I ran away. It was in Germany before the end of the war. I suppose he died, so many of them did—from starvation." She sighed.

Neal gave her a sympathetic look. "Well, I'm sure you can ride Pokey whenever you like. I'll speak to the Major about it."

"That would be like heaven," Illi said, urging Pokey ahead so she wouldn't have to look at Neal and that pitying look in his eyes.

Under her she could feel the controlled urgency of the horse and she wondered what he would do if she let him out. An old Arab saying that Geza had taught her came to her mind: Fleetest of foot is the chestnut, most enduring the bay, most spiritual the black, but most blessed the one with a white forehead. Well, this Pokey should be fleet and blessed, too.

They had come to a crossroads. Ahead, their own road widened and straightened, though it was still a dirt country road with a rocky crown. As if he had read her mind, Neal called, "Want to give Pokey his head a bit? It's safe here. I'll stay behind."

Illi called back, "I'll see what he can do," and they were off, Pokey well in the lead of Neal on his comfortable Rockabye. It felt so good, flying down the open stretch, the cool wind fanning her cheeks, her body one with the racing horse. She closed her eyes to savor the dream. Then she felt something was happening. Pokey reared suddenly on his hind legs and she leaned forward. His ears were laid back and he was letting out low, angry snorts. Just as suddenly he came down, circled, and gath-

ered himself to rear again. She tightened the reins, running her hand over his neck and speaking in low, comforting tones.

"There, there, Pokey. It is all right, boy." Then she saw what was frightening him. Pokey had heard it first. A car, small, tan-colored, was coming down the road toward them, going too fast for country driving. She could feel Pokey's tenseness and she knew he was watching the car, standing right in the middle of the road. Her heart leaped but she managed to boot him to one side in time to let the car pass. It was over quickly but not before she had seen the driver, Mark, grinning from ear to ear, and the white, frightened face of Ardis beside him.

She held Pokey there for a moment. He had stopped snorting but she could feel his trembling. Illi was trembling, too, but not from fright. She was angry. Why had Mark done a thing like that? He ought to know better than to take Ardis driving in that small, uncomfortable car, and to drive so fast. Even the Enwright station wagon in which she could ride, chair and all, always tired her. On the days when her father drove her over to the hospital for her treatment she usually came home and went straight to bed.

Illi felt a sharp stab of guilt. She shouldn't have left Ardis alone with Mark. Suddenly all the pleasure faded from the day. When Neal caught up to her she had Pokey already pointed toward home. He was angry, too.

"How are you? Are you all right?" he asked. "I should have told you that Pokey isn't used to cars yet. But I didn't think we'd meet anyone down this road. That crazy fool, whoever he is, was driving as if he were out on the Indianapolis speedway."

"Yes and I shall tell him so," Illi said, just as angrily.

"You know him?"

"Oh yes. He is Ardis' cousin. He is going to be living at the Enwrights' too. He arrived only yesterday."

"You don't sound happy about it. Don't you like him?"

"I have had no chance to like or dislike him," she said primly. "But most certainly I do not like what he has just done. I am going home now, Neal. But thank you for your kindness. I can see the stables some other day."

"But why? It's early yet."

"Yes, but I think I should be home when Ardis gets back. She will need me."

"Well, just as you say. I'll ride you up to the house and lead Pokey home from there."

"That is thoughtful of you. I am sorry I spoiled your day."

"Oh, I ought to be in studying anyway. Mr. Schmidt is giving me another German test next week. I don't want to flunk it again."

"I could help you, if you wanted me to," Illi offered.

"Would you? That would be great! But I don't want to impose on you," he added quickly and for some reason he looked decidedly uncomfortable.

"I would not mind, really," she assured him. "If you could bring your books over tonight . . . Ardis will probably go to bed early."

"I'll do that," he said. "But I'd like to meet that Ardis you think so much of. See you later then."

At the gate Illi swung herself from the saddle, drew the reins over Pokey's head, and handed them to Neal.

But he seemed reluctant to go. "You know," he said slowly, looking into her upturned, inquiring face, "you're the most surprising girl I have met for some time."

"Surprising? How?"

"Well, because you make me want to be honest with you. When I saw you sitting there on that rock yesterday, talking to yourself, I didn't think you were so much. You seemed terribly snooty."

"But you were waiting there in the same place today. Why?"

"Well, because after I'd talked to the Major I got an idea. He said you were German and as I needed some help I decided to—er—well—to get to know you."

"Oh. So? You were just—gold digging as Geegee would say?"

"Yeah, I guess that's about it. But don't get me wrong, Illi. I'm sorry I ever thought of it now. It isn't the German now—it's you. You've turned out to be such a different person since I know you better."

"It is the horse," Illi said with a toss of her bright head. "Horses always bring out the best in me."

"Now you're sore."

"No, not really. You did only what I would have done if I had needed help from someone. One takes what one can get in this world. Only—"

"Only what?"

"Only—" she gave him a shrewd look, "I would not have told on myself. But you did and it makes me feel better. It shows you are a nice person, much nicer than I am."

He gave a deep sigh of relief. "I don't know about the nice part but I'm glad we're friends, German or no German."

"But you will bring your books over tonight?"

"Yes, and thanks a lot, Illi."

He gave her a brief salute and was off down the drive. Illi went straight into the house to wait for Ardis.

She had her bed ready and warmed by the electric

blanket when she heard the car swoop up the drive, and a few moments later Mark stood in the doorway with a drooping Ardis in his arms. He looked pale and frightened, the way Janni had looked the day he had scared a horse with a slingshot and almost killed a young groom.

Mark laid Ardis gently on the couch. "She—she went all to pieces," he said helplessly to Illi. "I didn't know
. . ."

Illi could not scold him. She said, "She cannot stand much yet. Will you ask Mrs. Grimm to heat some milk —as usual?"

Mark left the room, glad to get away from Illi's cool, accusing look. And by the time Mrs. Grimm came hurrying in with a tray of hot milk and some crackers, Ardis was ready to be lifted into her bed under the warm covers.

"I wish I weren't such a sissy," she said to Illi as she nibbled on a cracker. "It was such a lovely day and Mark was so anxious to show off his new car . . . you wouldn't have let me go if you had been here, would you, Illi?"

"No, I would not. And Mark should have known better, or at least picked a better road," she said sharply. "Those ruts were throwing you from side to side. I thought you would be in the ditch any minute."

"Then it *was* you on that horse. I thought it was but I couldn't believe it. Whose horse was it, and who is the boy we passed on the road behind you?"

Illi told her. "He is coming over tonight to study. He wants to meet you but I said you would probably be in bed."

"To meet me?" Ardis seemed genuinely surprised. "Why?"

"I guess because I gave you such a—how is it they say? —building up?"

Ardis giggled. "Illi, you're so funny. You speak such beautiful English and then you come out with the funniest expressions."

"Do I?" Illi said stiffly. "You will have to excuse me. I am still not very good. Perhaps *I* should take lessons."

"But I'm not criticizing you, Illi. I love it, honestly I do. I—I love everything you do, Illi. It's always the right thing when it's for someone else. Like now, having this bed ready for me. I think I shall take a nap, so I can stay up tonight. And you go out and talk to poor Mark. I know I gave him a scare. He's not used to seeing me helpless like this."

Illi went out but Mark was nowhere to be found. She was glad he had disappeared. She wasn't sure she would have been as nice to him as Ardis would have wanted her to be. But Mark *muss gedemütigt werden*—how would Ardis say it? Oh yes, he must be "whittled down to size," and she would do the whittling.

Chapter 6

ARDIS WAS SITTING up bright and cheerful when Neal arrived that night. She insisted that Illi should bring him in to see her, and that the German lesson should be carried on in her room.

"Why can't I learn, too?" she'd asked. "My brain doesn't have to stop moving just because my legs have. If I can study other things with you, Illi, why can't I share the German lesson?"

Illi said there was no reason why she couldn't. She was so happy to see Ardis rested and full of good spirits after the shaking up she had had that afternoon. "Company is what she needs," she told herself. "Ardis needs to have a boy look at her the way Neal is doing. I guess every girl likes to see that sparkle of interest in a boy's eyes, no matter how helpless she is. It makes her feel pretty—and she *is* pretty," she thought, seeing Ardis in a new way.

Her lovely walnut-colored hair was brushed to a bright polish, her pretty hands moved gracefully in the air as she described something to Neal, her brown eyes were bright with excitement. Ardis may have been a freckled little tomboy three years ago when the polio had laid her low, but now with time to spend upon herself and her looks she was well on the way to being quite a beauty. Illi suspected that Ardis had often forced herself to care for her nails and her hair and her skin merely to bolster her courage, but now she might have another reason for it—a boy's admiration.

They were deep in the use of the dative case with certain verbs when Mark poked his head in the door.

"What goes on here?" he asked in a hurt, surprised way, as if he had been left out of something.

"Come in, Mark," Ardis called gaily. "You haven't met our neighbor, Neal Austin, yet. My cousin, Mark Williams."

Mark held out his hand and Neal took it politely if not cordially. "I saw you on that big roan today," Mark said. "Some horse." And turning to Ardis, "If you want me to leave, say so."

"No, he can stay if he behaves, can't he, Illi? We're getting a German lesson."

"He can stay. Perhaps he can help," Illi said. "You see, Neal, Mark has just come back from Germany. It may be that his German is better than mine, *das echte Hoch-*

deutsch—the real high German," she said pointedly. "I picked mine up in the streets and concentration camps. My French is far better."

"Gosh, do you know French, too, Illi?" Mark said eagerly. "I'm glad to hear that. French is my weak point. It may keep me out of college yet."

Illi raised her fine brows. "So? Now I have another pupil, *nicht wahr?* I must remember to tell Geegee I have found a better way to attract the boys." She gave Neal a sly look and smiled as his face turned a deep red.

"Oh, Illi!" Ardis seemed distressed. "Don't talk that way. You don't need German or French to attract the boys."

"I'll say she doesn't, not with that hair and that figure," said Mark. "How about it, Neal?" Illi thought that Mark was trying hard to win her favor. He must still be feeling guilty about the afternoon drive.

Neal cocked his head on one side, examining Illi as if she were a horse he was about to buy. "We-el," he drawled, "the hair is all right, but the figure, wouldn't you say *das Fräulein ist ein wenig fett?*—the girl is a little fat."

And now it was Illi's turn to grow red. "That may be true, but it is not very good German," she said and leafed through the book furiously.

Mark raised his brows at Neal, who winked at Ardis. She said, "They were only teasing, Illi. By the way, Mark, where have you been? Have you had your dinner?"

Mark shook his head. "I grabbed something over in town at the diner. I—well, I went over to sell my car, Ardis."

"Sell your car? But you just bought it. I thought you loved it. Why?"

"I got to thinking. You were right. It isn't quite the thing for the country. I picked up a jalopy, pretty beat up but cheap."

Illi raised her eyes from the German grammar in her lap and gave him a long, curious look. His eyes met hers and moved away. Mark wasn't telling the whole truth. He looked more than ever like Janni now, his eyes like a little boy's who has been caught in the cookie jar. She smiled and went back to the lesson in the book, for she knew what had happened. Mark had been scared. Ardis' collapse had taken some of the starch out of him, so maybe it was a good thing it had happened.

Then she heard him answering something Neal had asked. "Oh, I didn't lose anything on the deal. In fact when I traded in the Jag on the jalopy at another dealer's, they allowed me twenty dollars more than the original price."

"But I thought you were buying that Jag on time," Ardis said.

"I was—with a down payment, and I'm buying the jalopy that way, too, only it won't cost me so much to carry. A good deal all around. This is a sweet little car. Just wait until I get to work on it. All it needs is a ring job, maybe brake bands, and some new points."

Illi caught Neal's eyes. They were dancing with amusement. It was all right. He understood Mark, too, knew that he was whistling in the dark. She felt a lot better, as if they had all come a long way toward knowing each other, and listened with interest as Ardis explained that Mark had always been a fiend about motors and mechanics generally.

"Why Aunt Fran—that's Mark's mother—used to say she was afraid to move around the house. Something was always popping out at her, or bells were ringing or lights going on in unexpected places. Just like a House of Horrors in an amusement park. Mark could be a mechanical wizard if he tried."

"Who said I wasn't going to try?" Mark asked, half aggrieved. "That's what I came home for. If they can ever get my credits straightened out, I want to get into college and major in science and then onto engineering school."

"But I thought—surely you'll be going to West Point like your father," Ardis exclaimed.

Mark shook his head. "Not me. I had a hard time talking the old man out of it but I finally did. I've seen enough of what war can do. I'd like to build up rather than tear down."

"Who wouldn't?" Neal put in quickly. "But there may have to be some more tearing down before we're ready for your brave new world, Mark. I hope not, but I'm going to be ready for it."

Illi looked from one boy to the other, so different, each with his sights set in a different direction, and yet both right in a way because they were both so sincere. A respect for Mark began to replace the antagonism he had first aroused in her. He didn't seem so much like the arrogant young man of the world now. His hair was mussed and there was a smudge on one cheek. Maybe he would turn out to be a welcome addition to the En-

67

wright household. Maybe there would be room for them both.

Silence hung over the group for a minute as each pursued the ideas the boys' remarks had brought forth. Then Ardis broke it. "Haven't we had enough German for tonight, Illi?" she asked.

"Of course. What would you like to do?" Illi closed the book and handed it to Neal.

"I'd like the boys to build a big fire in the living-room fireplace and then come back and wheel me in there, and then you and Mark can go downstairs and find something exciting to eat. Maybe we could toast cheese sandwiches and pop corn."

And so the lesson turned into a party, and it was thus that Mrs. Enwright found them when she and her husband came home earlier than usual.

"How cozy!" she exclaimed, throwing her coat on a chair. Illi went to pick it up. She thought, as she always did, how everything changed when pretty, vivacious *Mütterchen* came into a room. The fire seemed to burn brighter, the voices rose higher, even the clock ticked more busily.

She went over to kiss Ardis and then warmed her fingers over the fire. "Now this is what I like to see. Have you some food for Daddy and me?"

Mark bent to toast two more sandwiches and Neal was presented.

"Oh yes, I know all about you," Mrs. Enwright said cordially. "Why haven't you been to see us before?"

"I guess I've been too busy for visiting," Neal said.

"Yes, the Major says you're studying hard. He thinks you're going to be God's gift to the American Army some day."

"Oh no!" Neal burst out in honest laughter. "He was just stringing you, Mrs. Enwright."

"No, he says you have a natural way of cutting through difficulties and getting things done. He's watched you with the grooms and the stable boys and they all snap to it when you appear. But maybe I shouldn't be telling you all this."

"Oh, Neal knows how to make people work for him, you're right, *Mütterchen*," Illi said with a wicked glance at Neal.

"Now, Illi, for that you're going to have to eat this lovely charcoal marshmallow," he said, and coming over he popped a burnt one into her mouth. Illi sputtered and everybody laughed.

"But for our Princess over there on her throne I shall toast the most beautiful brown one, succulent, bubbling —" he thrust a stick in the fire and twirled it over the flames.

Mrs. Enwright smiled and came to plump the pillow behind Ardis, who was beginning to sag. "Only one more, Neal," she said, "and then I think the Princess had better retire. She has had a big day, so I've been told. I hope you'll come over again soon, however. We like company."

"Oh, yes, please do," Ardis echoed her mother. "We're going to have Geegee over to spend the night soon."

"Who's Geegee?" asked Mark.

"Who's Geegee?" Neal started to laugh. "You

wouldn't be asking that if you'd been around here long. Everyone knows Geegee, don't they, Illi?"

"Geegee is fun," Illi said cautiously.

"Of course she's fun and pretty, too. Cute as a button. And a smooth dancer," Neal added.

"I thought you said you didn't dance," Ardis said with a wistful look in her eyes.

"I don't, not this year," Neal said. "This year I'm a hermit and Geegee isn't interested in hermits."

"Well, I'm no hermit," Mark said. "Bring on your Geegee. She sounds good."

"Maybe she won't ride in a stripped-down jalopy," Ardis said.

"Jalopy?" Mrs. Enwright seemed surprised. "I heard a different story from Mrs. Grimm, or am I mistaken?"

"You heard right, Aunt Mims, but I sold the de luxe job later this afternoon," he said. "I was afraid it would get me into trouble."

"Well, I'm glad to hear that," Mrs. Enwright said, and, turning Ardis' chair, she said good night and wheeled her off to bed. Illi did not offer to go along. She knew that this was a labor of love that Mrs. Enwright liked to do by herself.

"Want me to run you over?" Mark asked as Neal started to gather up his books.

"No, I'd rather walk. It's a nice night. Couldn't you stand some fresh air?" he asked Illi, who nodded and went for her coat.

The night was still, with an orange hunter's moon rising over the hill. The frost in the air gave it a fine nippy feeling. As they talked they could see their breaths making clouds before them.

70

"Well?" Illi spoke first. "How did you like Ardis?"

"She's pretty special, isn't she? You know at first I could have cried seeing her sitting there, looking just like any girl you might want to ask to a dance—and not being able to."

"But you must not treat her that way, Neal. You must act as if she is just like any other girl. That is what the doctors say. It is important for her to feel normal."

"Oh, I soon got over that first feeling. Ardis isn't going to let anyone shed tears for her, not even herself. She's a good sport if there ever was one."

"Yes, she is," Illi agreed. "And now maybe you will understand, Neal, why I feel the way I do about Ardis and why I may not be able to do certain things when you ask me to. I could never let her down."

"Ye-es, I understand, but I do think you take it too seriously, Illi. After all you're not her nurse, you know. They don't expect *that* of you. I could see that by the way Mrs. Enwright treated you. What was it you called her?"

"*Mütterchen.* You should know what that means: little mother. I had to call her something that would show her how I felt about her. I'm still a little afraid of her, afraid I might be a disappointment to her, and I admire her so much. I am grateful, Neal, for all this, but it is so hard to say it sometimes." She waved her hand toward the lighted house behind them and the woods and meadows that lay on each side of the small stream that caught the moonlight like a tinsel ribbon.

Neal shifted his books and, moving closer, felt for her hand. He gave it a tight squeeze. "You want to know something?" he said. "I think you're wonderful, too, just as wonderful and brave as Ardis. When I think of all you've been through—oh yes, Ardis told me about you—I think it's pretty fine the way you've kept that spunky little chin of yours up." He cuffed it gently. "I didn't know there were any girls like you two, and I'm glad I know you both. So long, see you tomorrow."

She waved him off and stood watching as he swung down the road. Then she turned and went up the lane to the house, drawing in deep breaths of the sharp air. It felt good to be alive tonight, alive and in America where people were kind and thoughtful like the Enwrights and Neal—and even Mark.

She could hear voices in the living room as she passed through the hall on her way to her room, and would have kept on if Mrs. Enwright had not called to her.

"Come in, Illi," she said and moved over to make room for her on the davenport. Mr. Enwright was standing before the fire, puffing away on his pipe, and Mark sat sprawled in a big chair facing him, a serious look on his face. Illi sensed that Mark had been hearing a few things he didn't like. He looked like Janni when her father scolded him for some boyish prank. She couldn't help feeling sorry for him.

"We've been discussing Mark's plans for college," Mrs. Enwright said. "We've found out he can still register as a day student for Bartram College, just twenty miles the other side of town. They have a fine science department there. They will accept all his foreign credits except his French. Mark doesn't want to ask you, but I was wondering if you could help him with that?"

"Of course," Illi said. She smiled at Mark, who eyed

her suspiciously. "I'll do what I can. I can't speak it but I can read it fairly well."

"Where did you study it?" Mr. Enwright asked with interest.

"My mother was teaching me when—before things began to happen. She knew four languages," she said proudly. "All well-educated people do over there. I could read right through my French story book. It had been hers, such a lovely book. La Fontaine's Fables, all illustrated by Gustave Doré." Now why had she remembered that? But she was remembering a lot of things lately. She felt as if she were unfolding inside like a flower, petal after petal. She could see the interest mounting in Mr. Enwright's eyes.

"I know that book," he said. "They are getting rare nowadays." He reached down and took her hand. "You come along with me a moment. I have something to show you."

She went with him to his study and stood waiting while he searched the shelves for something.

"It's here, I know it is," he kept murmuring. "I saw it just the other day."

"I don't see how you can find anything," Illi laughed. "And it would take such a little bit of doing to put it all in order."

"Sometime, sometime," he said vaguely. Then he picked a book from a shelf and blew the dust off the top. "Here it is. Was your book like this?"

Illi held it in her hands as if it were something that might blow away like ashes if she moved too quickly.

"It is the very one," she said quietly and laid it gently on the desk so she could turn the pages.

73

"Well, that answers a question for me," Mr. Enwright said. "Now I know why I bought it. It wasn't for Ardis, she's too old for fairy tales and I don't go in for French books. I must have had second sight and known you were coming to live with us. You better take it up to your room before it gets lost again."

"Oh!" Illi said, so overcome she could hardly speak. It was like meeting an old friend. Then she did a curious thing, something she'd never have done if she'd stopped to think about it. She threw her arms around Mr. Enwright's neck and gave him a sound kiss on his cheek. "Thank you, thank you, Daddy Bill," she half sobbed.

Mr. Enwright took off his glasses and polished them busily. "Well, let's not cry about it," he said with a pleased smile. "And let me say I like that Daddy Bill business. I've been sort of jealous of *Mütterchen* for some time."

"I have been calling you that in my mind," Illi told him, "only it has been so hard to say it."

"Well, now that it's said, let's keep it up," he said, patting her shoulder in a comfortable way. "By the way, how would you like to straighten out this mess for me? Not all at once but in your spare time?"

"You mean you'd trust me?" Illi asked in surprise.

"Yes, I think I can. I like the way you handle books."

Mark was leaving for his roost in the barn when they went back to the living room, Illi's eyes like sapphires and the book under her arm clutched tight.

"Good night everybody," he said. "I'm off for the polar regions. Wish me luck!"

"I'm sorry we haven't been able to get your room

74

fixed yet, Mark," Mrs. Enwright said. "You can sleep here on the davenport, if you like."

Mark shrugged and said he guessed he could take it, but when he went into the hall Illi followed him.

"Look, Mark," she said, "I'll swap with you. You can have my room. I don't mind the barn a bit. In fact I like barns. I'm used to them."

"Why of course I won't swap," he said brusquely. "What do you think I am?"

"But it doesn't seem fair when you belong here and I—"

"Belong? Who belongs more than you, I'd like to know." There was a bitterness in his voice, and Illi knew he was still smarting from the going-over Mr. and Mrs. Enwright had given him. Perhaps finding his place in America and in this home was not going to be easy for Mark either. She wanted to help him, but this was not the time.

She said good night and went slowly up the stairs to her own comfortable little room. She had a lot to think about. It had been a full day, a big day in more ways than one. She felt as if she had come a long distance in a short time. Why she could even look back now without any regret or bitterness in her heart!

Chapter 7

SATURDAY THAT WEEK was rainy, and usually Illi would have spent it with Mrs. Grimm or in Ardis' room sewing, doing nails, or studying. But this morning after doing her own room she put on a scarf and a raincoat, and sticking her head in Ardis' door said, "Can you manage without me for a little while?"

"Of course," Ardis said and then waving a letter at her, "it's from my friend, Peg Darcy. She's made the nicest sorority at State." Ardis kept up a large correspondence with her old city friends who were now scattered in boarding school or college.

"Sorority? What is that?" Illi asked, coming into the room.

"A sort of club—for girls. It's usually a big thing for a girl to be asked to join one."

"Oh! And how do they pick the ones who are asked?" Illi put the question with great interest.

"Well, they usually pick the most popular or the richest or the prettiest or the best athlete or a girl whose mother or sisters have belonged to the same sorority. Sometimes they pick the brainiest girls, but *they* don't usually care much about sororities. They—why are you frowning? Oh, I see, you think this is snobbish."

"Is it not?"

Ardis was thoughtful. "I suppose it is in a way, but I'd never thought about it like that. A lot of schools have abolished them." She laughed uneasily. "You're picking another hole in our democratic way of life, aren't you?"

Illi shook her head. "It is all very puzzling. I am told that here everyone is alike, and then I find it is not so."

"Of course it isn't so. People *can't* be alike. There will always be leaders and followers and doers and thinkers. But we do believe that everyone here has a chance to make the most of what he's got. I think that's part of democracy, don't you?"

"Perhaps. But those girls—the ones who are not asked. How do they feel?" She had sympathy for the rejected ones of this world.

"I don't think it means that much to most of them," Ardis said. "A sorority doesn't mean anything very important. It's a house to live in and a lot of fun. And the girls who want to join generally get into one even if it isn't the one they'd choose."

"Well, that is one decision I shall not have to make," Illi said on her way to the door.

"Why not? I bet every sorority in the college will be fighting for you," Ardis assured her.

"But I may not go to college."

"You can if you want to. Daddy and Mother have said you could, you know."

"I know, but there may be something I shall want to do more than that," Illi said mysteriously and ducked out the door before Ardis could question her further.

She wasn't ready yet to share her dreams, to tell some of the things that Miss Patchin had told her a few days ago. She had said that Illi had an unusually good sense of design and a feeling for color and good materials. She'd said Illi should be thinking of making a career of fashion design, that she might be able to get a scholarship for one of the good schools. She had thanked Miss Patchin for her interest, but she had not told her that her mother had been a well-known portrait painter in Hungary and so why shouldn't she have some artistic leanings? It would have sounded like bragging.

But Miss Patchin's talk had given her some ideas. She didn't know yet just how she wanted to use this gift she seemed to have inherited, or how the next year would be for her. If Ardis improved as the doctors seemed to think she would, Illi would be free to go on with her own career; but if not, her place was here with Ardis. But she could afford to put her decision off until her senior year. Now she had something else to do.

She went out into the sharp, damp morning. The rain had turned to a misty fog through which the autumn colors showed only faintly. She wondered what Neal would be doing this morning. There would be no riding today. It should give him a good chance to make some progress with his German—if he would. That was one thing she found it hard to understand about the American boys and girls. They were so easy-going, most of them. They had all the opportunities for success handed to them and mostly for nothing, but they did not appreciate them. They did not make the most of these opportunities. Maybe it was because everything was made too easy for them. They did not know what really hard work meant. Even in the old days at home in Budapest, Janni and she had had to study hard. At fifteen Janni would have been ready for college in this country.

Thinking of Janni she drew a deep sigh. It was the one thing from her past she could not forget, because she was not sure that there was a Janni any more. How he would have loved it here! How he and Neal would have got on together in their common love of horses!

She stepped across the wet side yard to the barn, looking for Mark. Mrs. Grimm had said he'd had his breakfast early and gone off. This would be a good day to get him started on that French. She peeped into the garage but there was no jalopy. On impulse she made her way to the upper barn, up some steps cut into the bank, and around to the big barn door through which the hay wagons used to drive. Where the cows had been kept on the lower level was now garage and storage space. She went in through the small door that was cut in the huge barn door. It was quiet inside except for the cooing of the pigeons. It smelled of old hay but it was clean and not too cold. She went over to the corner where a room had been boarded off for keeping the grain. She tapped on the door and when there was no answer went inside.

Mark's new quarters were appallingly empty. There was nothing in the room but an army cot, an old wicker chair, and a shelf on which his personal possessions were scattered. His clothes hung from some pegs on the wall. It looked as dreary in the gray light as one of the cells in a concentration camp. She wondered how long it would be before the Enwrights would fix it up for him and if this was part of the discipline they felt he needed. It wouldn't be so bad if there were a rug on the floor and curtains at the windows.

She went back to the house, going in by her own door, to the chest in her room where she rooted among the old things Mrs. Enwright had told her she might use. There she found some old monk's cloth curtains which would have to be shortened, and she took them

back to the barn to measure them. She was perched precariously on the arm of the wicker chair when she heard steps crossing the barn floor. They came to stop at the door.

"Illi! What on earth are you doing?" It was Mrs. Enwright.

"Just measuring some curtains for this window. I thought Mark's room looks so cold and cheerless . . ."

"So you've taken him under your wing, too?" Mrs. Enwright came into the room and held out a helping hand to Illi.

"Well, I felt sorry for him. He has to get used to a lot of new things. It is not easy, I know that."

"No it isn't easy, especially for a boy like Mark. I suppose you think we are hard on him, Illi, making him live in a place like this, fussing about that car he bought . . ."

"Oh, I think you were right—about the car," Illi said quickly. "I think he was just showing off."

"Exactly. Mark has always been a smart boy, way ahead of his age, and living the way army children do, here today gone tomorrow, he—well he just got too big for his breeches as we say here."

"*Ein Grossprahler?*"

Mrs. Enwright smiled. "A bragger? Maybe. His father was too strict with him and his mother too easy. So Mark has grown up something of a problem. It got to the point in Germany—well, you can imagine how the girls went for a handsome American boy like that."

Illi had no trouble imagining. She had seen a lot of it when she was living with Mrs. Lyons.

"I've always been fond of Mark, my sister knows that,

81

but she knows I can be strict. So it's up to me, in fact to all of us to get him straightened out. That's why I asked you to help, Illi. You have such a straight way of thinking and you see through people so well. So I'm asking you, don't spoil Mark. He has fine stuff in him. We want to bring it out."

"Oh, I am sure he has," Illi agreed. "But would it be spoiling him to fix up this room—just a little?"

Mrs. Enwright laughed. "I can see your fingers are itching to get to it. Go ahead. There's a lot of stuff in the attic you can use, but be sure to make Mark help you. We've been in town buying a shower bath and other fixings to put in here, but Mark's Uncle Bill is going to make Mark do most of the work. That will keep him busy."

"And don't forget the French," Illi reminded her.

"I'm not worrying too much about that," Mrs. Enwright said. "Mark has had a good many years of it, he should be able to make the grade at Bartram. I just wanted to make it seem hard for him. I think he had an idea he could come over here and sail right in, no exams, nothing. I must go now and get Ardis ready for her treatment. Oh, by the way—I've been thinking next week is Halloween. It's a great party time in this country. Do you suppose we could get a few young people together for a party, right here in the barn?"

"We could ask Geegee and Neal—"

"And Tom Grimm will be home on leave. I think it would be good for Ardis."

"It would, indeed," Illi agreed. "I never saw her so—so full of good spirits as she was last night. She likes company."

82

"Do you think Neal Austin had anything to do with it?" Mrs. Enwright asked slyly.

"Maybe. He likes her, you know, he told me so. *Mütterchen*, tell me, will Ardis really be able to use her legs and dance again like any other girl?"

A shadow passed over Mrs. Enwright's pretty face. "We are hoping so, and praying for it. The doctors say it is possible. They are making such progress with polio and of course we are doing everything we can to help. I believe the best thing we did, Illi, was sending for you. We'll be eternally in your debt for what you've done for Ardis. She was beginning to droop like a little flower before you came—and now look at her!"

"I love her," Illi said simply. "I would do anything in the world for her."

"I believe you would, but don't do too much. We don't want you to feel that you are chained to Ardis' chair. You've got to get out and lead a normal life of your own, you know. What about that horse Ardis was telling me about? Do you like to ride?"

Illi's face broke into a radiant smile. "I love it. *Mütterchen*, how much would a little horse like that cost to buy? He is not registered, you know. Neal says the Major will probably not keep him long."

Mrs. Enwright's eyes clouded. "I have no idea, Illi. But I'm afraid we couldn't afford any kind of a horse right now."

"Oh, please, I did not mean for *you* to buy it. I was just thinking if I had the money myself . . . there are ways I could make it. There will be a vacancy in the Elite Dress Shop after school and on Saturdays, and with Mark here . . ."

83

Mrs. Enwright leaned over and took her hand. "Be patient, Illi. We're willing to do anything we can to make you happy, but we don't want you to think of going out to earn money yet. We need you here, Illi. Ardis needs you. Mark could never take your place with her."

Illi nodded and gulped down the lump in her throat.

"I'll see if we can stretch your allowance a little."

"Oh, please, I didn't mean that either. I was just—how do you say it?—window-shopping? I was just so afraid the Major might sell Pokey and I wouldn't see him any more. But Neal says it is all right for me to ride him. He wants me to ride over to Norwood with him tomorrow if it is nice. Would it be all right, do you think, *Mütterchen?*"

"To Norwood? Isn't that where the Prentices live?"

"Yes, I believe so. They are friends of Major Wallace's. They have some fine horses, Neal says."

"And a lot of money. We should send you off in style. Now let's see—" Mrs. Enwright narrowed her eyes. "Turn around, Illi. Yes, I believe they would fit. When you go up to the attic to look for things for the room here, take a look in that cedar closet. I think I have an old pair of jodhpurs and a jacket in there. Maybe even a pair of boots. I used to ride, too, before I was married. If they fit, you can wear them."

"Oh, they will fit," Illi cried, "I shall make them fit! And thank you, *Mütterchen*, thank you for everything."

Chapter 8

MRS. ENWRIGHT MUST have been much thinner before she was married, Illi thought, surveying her figure in her mirror in the trim riding breeches, for they fit almost perfectly now that she'd let out the back seam. The boots were a little long in the foot, but by stuffing the toes with cotton they would do. But the jacket was impossible, too narrow across the shoulders and too nipped-in at the waist. However, with a tan sweater and a gay scarf at her throat Illi felt she could make her riding outfit do.

"I am used to left-overs and hand-me-downs. I can still take things and be thankful," she told herself in the mirror a bit wistfully. She remembered the day after

85

she had arrived and *Mütterchen* had rushed her off in a taxi to a big store and had outfitted her completely from head to toe. It was the first time for years that she had had anything of her own and it had been hard to believe.

The sun was shining brightly and warmly outside, and though it was too early for Neal to come, she wanted to go out and enjoy the day. She stood at the top of the stairs, hesitating whether to go down and show herself off to Ardis, then decided against it. It might make Ardis feel too badly to see her going off on a jaunt with Neal. So she went out her own door and down the hill to the drive.

Mark was in the barn yard working on his jalopy. Another boy in uniform was with him and they were both bending over the motor, which seemed to be making a terrific racket. The car was the worst she had ever seen. It looked as if it were held together with wire coat hangers and bits of string. The stuffing was coming out of the upholstery, the paint was off the fenders, and the glass in one door was cracked.

Mark looked up and saw her, and reaching into the engine he turned something that cut off the noise.

"Hi!" he said. "How do you like her?" There was oil on his hands and a smudge on his face, but Illi thought he had never looked so happy nor so pleasant.

"Very fine, if she goes better than she looks," Illi said.

"Oh, she will. She's not much now, but wait. Tom's going to show me how to soup her up, aren't you, Tom?"

"You bet," Tom said and held out a hand to Illi. "I haven't met you yet, but I've heard plenty about you from Mom. She thinks you are just about all right."

"You must be Tom Grimm," Illi said, returning the friendly grasp of his hand. "I know somebody whom your mother thinks is perfect. She talks of you every hour on the hour." She liked this Tom Grimm's looks, tall and rangy, with a nose a little too big and ears that stood out too much, but nice, oh, very nice.

"You know how mothers are," Tom said a little sheepishly. "If I were around all the time it would be another story."

"But now you are her hero. You are going to save America, singlehanded."

Tom's eyes twinkled. "Hardly. Unless doing KP is heroic. I'm out of boot camp next week though. I think they're going to move me on to the Air Force, as I asked."

"You mean you are going to be a flier?" Mark asked.

"No, I'm going in for aviation mechanics."

"But don't you want to fly?" Illi asked in her turn.

"Oh, I don't know. I'd just as soon stick with the ground crew. Somebody has to do the dirty work and I'm not going to make a career of this business. I got to get home as soon as I can and help Mom out with the other kids." He turned back to the car. "Now what you want to do with this crate, Mark, is to get a whole new wiring system. If you don't you're going to have trouble —see?" He yanked a wire which came apart in his hands. "If you get the wire I'll help you with it while I'm home this week."

"But unfortunately Mark ought to be working on his French this week, or he won't be able to keep up in his class at Bartram."

87

"You're beginning to talk like a schoolmarm already," Mark said, wiping his hands on his good gray flannels.

Illi leaned over and picked up an old cloth hanging from a bush. "Here," she said, "this is better. I think you need a nursemaid, too."

"Want the job?" Mark taunted her.

"I should say not, I have more interesting things to do," Illi said with a toss of her head like Geegee.

Mark and Tom both laughed. "She's learning quickly, isn't she?" Mark said. "I bet she's off for a date with Neal." He gave Tom a wink. "That's a case of 'love my horse, love me.'"

"It is nothing of the sort," Illi said, but she could feel a slow flush mounting to her cheeks. "We have been invited to the Prentices'—that is, the Major and Neal were and the Major told Neal to bring me."

"The Prentices!" Tom gave a low whistle. "Moving in society, aren't you?"

"Am I? I do not know. We are going over to look at some new horses they have just bought, that is all."

"Well, give the horses my love," Mark said and stooped to the engine again. "Want me to give you a lift over to the Major's?"

"No, thank you. Neal is coming for me." She turned and went slowly down the lane, conscious that two pairs of interested eyes were upon her.

She had reached the Wallace gate without meeting Neal but as she hesitated there she heard them coming, Neal on Rockabye and leading Pokey.

"There she is, Pokey," he said, seeing her. "The pretty girl in the tan sweater. Remember her?"

"Hi, Pokey! *Gyere ide!*" she called as she had called before. Pokey came running and stopped close to nuzzle her hands for the sugar she had brought him.

"He knows me," Illi said delightedly.

"Of course he does. How could he forget you? You're not the forgettable kind, Illi."

"Thank you." She made him a mocking bow and swung to the saddle.

They ambled along comfortably, the sun warm on their backs, the leaves sifting down on them in a multicolored rain.

"Those Prentices, are they society?" she asked Neal suddenly.

"Well, you might call them that, but they don't put on airs, if that's what you mean. They have plenty of money, but about all they care about is horses—like you and me." He gave her a broad grin. "They're great friends of the Major's and sometimes Peachy—that's the girl—asks me over for a double date. I had to refuse her the last couple of times though. I'm too busy."

"Peachy! What a queer name!"

"It's really Marian. But Peachy suits her. She's a cute kid. She can ride anything that runs on four legs."

From behind them they could hear the clop of hoofs and Illi looked back to see the Major on his black mare catching up with them.

"Well," he said as he drew in his horse, "she does know how to ride, doesn't she?" He gave Illi an approving look. "Neal has been singing your praises. He tells me Pokey has taken quite a shine to you."

"Yes, and I to him," Illi said eagerly. She was losing some of her fear of the Major. "Maybe it is because he is so much like a horse I used to have back home in Hungary."

"Hungary, eh?" The Major bunched his thick red eyebrows. "So you're from Hungary. Fine country. They used to raise some fine specimens of horseflesh over there before the war."

"I know. My grandfather ran one of the large breeding farms—it was called Kisber. Maybe you have heard of it?"

"Kisber." The Major's blue eyes, looking bluer than ever in his wind-beaten face, were focused straight ahead. Illi wondered if he'd forgotten her completely. Then he said, "I wonder what happened to all those horses. Do you know?"

"I know the Germans took them into Germany so the Russians would not get them, because I went with them. But after that—well, I never heard. I suppose most of them died from starvation and neglect. They were beginning to die off when—when I left the remount station after my grandfather was taken away—" she stopped because she couldn't go on. She couldn't talk about that last day when the soldiers had taken Grandfather Laszlos away and in her loneliness and fright she too had run away, or about the night when she had gone to say good-by to Vidám in his stall.

"Well now," the Major said awkwardly, "that's past and gone. You'll find some good horses over here. What was this horse of yours like?"

"Oh, he was a chestnut thoroughbred with a lot of Arabian in him—with the same markings that Pokey has."

The Major chuckled. "This little fellow has a lot of

Arabian in him, I imagine. Look at the deep dish, the bulging gibah, the large, wide-spaced eyes, the small ears."

As if he knew he were being discussed, Pokey threw up his head in an interested way, pawing the ground restlessly.

"Go ahead, let him out," the Major said. "I'll meet you there."

At the crossroads they turned right and were soon drawing up at another gate, with a Kentucky gate opener, which they could operate without dismounting, leading to a drive that led to the paddock. A girl was standing there watching them approach. She was quite small with a head of close curls and a figure that was neat and showed off to perfection in her well-cut riding clothes. She had apparently just come in, for a groom was leading off a sweating horse.

"Don't let him stand a minute, Simmy," she called to him. "And take a look at that right shoe." Then she came sauntering up as Neal swung to the ground. "Hi, Neal!" She made a telescope of her hands and peered through them comically. "It *is* Neal, isn't it? I expected to see a long beard, to here," she indicated his waistline.

To Illi he said, "Don't mind Peachy. She dramatizes everything. This is Illi Horvath, Peachy Prentice. You two ought to have a lot in common to talk about."

"Meaning you?" Peachy asked saucily.

"No, I mean horses, Little One. Illi loves them, too."

"Oh yes, of course, horses," Peachy said, but she gave Illi a thorough going-over between one blink of her thick eyelashes and the next. She missed nothing, and Illi in her hand-me-down pants felt awkward and embarrassed. "Is that your horse?" Peachy asked, coming over to examine Pokey.

"No, he belongs to the Major but—I wish he were. I have no horse of my own—here."

"Here? You mean you have horses at home?"

"Illi's home was in Hungary, before the war," Neal put in quickly, sensing Illi's discomfort. "But she lives here now, with the Enwrights."

"Oh." Peachy seemed to have lost interest. She walked over to inspect Pokey closely. "He's a darling," she said. "Where did he come from, Neal?"

"I don't know, you'll have to ask the Major. He'll be along in a moment."

"I'll do that," Peachy said and led the way to the stables. "I suppose you want to see what we've got. Dad went overboard this time. But I don't think he picked up anything as nice as that Pokey."

Illi felt herself stiffen. That girl, she thought, wants Pokey. Well, she won't get him. I'd die if she did.

By the end of the afternoon when they had toured the Prentice stables and were having tea in the living room that was as big as a ballroom, she was sure of it. She liked Mr. Prentice. He was a jolly, energetic, forthright man. Peachy was a lot like him. But her brother, Phil, a year older, was more like Mrs. Prentice, pale, quiet, not interested in horses at all. He spent most of the afternoon in a chair off by himself in a corner with a book. Illi found herself alone with Mrs. Prentice, who could talk of nothing but the weather and how she wished Peachy would wear warmer clothes when she went riding. Illi was glad when she excused herself and she was free to join Neal and Peachy who were bent over the shelf of records in a corner. But when she stepped up to them she could hear that they were in a heated argument.

"Honest, Peachy," Neal was saying, "I'm telling you the truth. I've turned over a new leaf. I can't play around. I'm too busy with the horses and my studies—here, ask Illi. She knows."

Peachy darted a quick glance at Illi, but she did not ask the question. She said with an impatient toss of her curly head, "It isn't important. Let's talk about the colt. What's his full name?"

"Hocus-pocus," said Neal, evidently glad that the conversation had taken a change. "We call him Pokey."

"I'm going to ask the Major about him right away," Peachy said and went across to where her father and the Major were deep in horse talk.

Illi watched her go with a sinking heart. "Neal," she whispered, "do you think the Major would let her have Pokey?"

"I don't know. Depends upon Mr. Prentice. Let's get in on this." He took her by the hand and led her over to the others.

"But you must see him, Daddy," Peachy was saying. "He's a darling. Where did you say you got him, Major?"

"I didn't say, young lady," Major Wallace said, his blue eyes twinkling.

"Which means he isn't saying," her father laughed. "That right, Jim?"

"We-el," began the Major, but Peachy interrupted impatiently:

"But you must know. He must have papers."

"That's the hitch. He hasn't."

"Oh." Peachy was disappointed. "Dad would never let me buy anything without papers, would you, Daddy?"

"That depends what you want him for," her father said. "Let's take a look at this wonder horse."

They all went out together to the paddock and waited while the groom went to bring Pokey to them.

"Call him," Neal whispered.

Illi's lips were dry, but as he appeared around the corner of the stables she managed to get out, "Here, Pokey! *Gyere ide!*"

Pokey came running straight to her and waited for his sugar.

"What did she say?" Peachy asked.

"It's Hungarian. It means 'Come here!' " Neal told her.

Illi did not miss the look which the Major and Mr. Prentice exchanged.

"He seems to understand you," Mr. Prentice said.

"Yes, I think we have established a—what can I call it?—an *entente?*" Illi was smiling but inside she was not so happy.

"You say you got him in Maryland?" Mr. Prentice asked the Major as he walked around Pokey to examine his conformation.

"Yes, a friend of mine gave him to me for a favor I'd done him. And one doesn't look a gift horse in the mouth, does one?" the Major said drily.

"No, I suppose not. I hear some of those German horses the Army brought back to the remount station in Virginia found homes in Maryland. Is that so?"

"Perhaps," the Major said shortly.

"There was some hush-hush about it, I know," Mr. Prentice went on. "Thoroughbreds without papers, contrabands of war, 'wild horses' I think they were called."

Illi's ears were pricking like Pokey's. Contrabands of war. Could it mean that some of those horses she had known had survived the German neglect and were here in this country?

On the way home she asked the Major, "What is a 'wild horse,' Major Wallace?"

"It's a name they sometimes give to horses with no proof of ownership. The Jockey Club does not recognize their foals even if the owner knows exactly where they came from. It's a gap in their registered history, you see. Their get are only half-breds."

"Oh. Would a colt of such a horse be valuable?"

"Not for breeding. He might be valuable otherwise."

"Where did these horses Mr. Prentice spoke of come from?"

The Major looked a little troubled. "It's no secret, but it is not too well known that some of our officers brought back from Germany some abandoned thoroughbreds they found there. They were sent to our army remount station in Virginia but when the Russians found out about them they put up a squawk, saying they really belonged to them. So we got rid of them quickly, to avoid a fuss. Or that's what I've been told. I couldn't swear to it."

"But why did the Russians claim them?"

"Because they had conquered Hungary and the horses were Hungarian." The Major seemed to be watching

95

Illi's face. "Now see here, my dear, don't you get any farfetched ideas in your head. I wasn't going to tell you this until I did some investigating—"

"But you will, you will try to find out where Pokey came from? If his sire or dam was one of those horses . . ." Illi could hardly speak she was so full of the possibilities the Major's words had brought up.

"Yes, I'll see what I can find out," the Major promised. "But it may take some time. My friend who owned him is away in Europe. But I'll do my best." He smiled in an assuring way at Illi and she wondered how she could have been so afraid of him before.

"And you will not sell him to Peachy Prentice?" she dared to ask.

The Major's eyes crinkled with amusement. "Now *that* I can't promise. There's no telling what a cute little girl like Peachy will do to get around an old man like me," he teased.

"I—I could get around an old man, too, if he was as nice and kind as you," Illi laughed softly. "Please, Major, I'd die if I couldn't see Pokey now and then. You see he's sort of like me—no papers, no proof of origin. I guess we're both 'wild horses.' I think that is why we took to each other so quickly."

"Okay, okay, don't cry," the Major said uncomfortably as Illi brushed away some tears. "I have no intention of selling the colt to anyone at the moment. I want to see how he works out. Ride him when you want, only don't go out alone. I don't trust him yet. He's an unpredictable little cuss, Neal says."

"*I* shall always know what he is going to do," Illi said proudly. "We understand each other, don't we, Pokey?"

Chapter 9

IT HAD BEEN decided to invite Peachy and her brother for the Saturday Halloween party, but Illi had refused to do the calling up.

"But why?" Ardis had asked. "You know them and I don't."

"I would rather not," Illi said stubbornly. "This Peachy makes me feel uncomfortable. I know she does not like me. I am afraid she would not come."

Ardis frowned. "There you go again, Illi. I thought you'd got over that—suspecting everyone. It's so silly. Everyone likes you when you'll let them. The trouble with you is that you pull in your head like a snapping turtle. Why wouldn't Peachy like you?"

Illi shook her head. She couldn't tell Ardis what she suspected, that Peachy wouldn't like anyone whom Neal seemed to like. She was sure that Peachy's sudden desire to possess Pokey was just a part of her jealousy.

In the end it was Mrs. Enwright who invited the Prentices. Illi found herself dreading the party which at first she had looked forward to with so much pleasure. Geegee had come over early on Saturday to help Illi and the boys get the barn ready, and already Mark and she had gone off together in the jalopy to gather up some cornstalks and pumpkins from a neighboring farm.

Tom and Illi were left alone to sweep and string up the electric bulbs and bring out the chairs and the record player. In the kitchen Mrs. Enwright was helping Mrs. Grimm with the refreshments. Ardis wheeled herself excitedly back and forth through the house making lists. She'd found an old book of Halloween customs and insisted they were going to try them all.

"This is a fine thing for Ardis," Tom said, reaching with the broom for a big cobweb that hung from a beam. "She was a lonely little girl until you came, Illi. I can see the improvement already. I'm a great believer in mind over body—if you know what I mean."

Illi nodded. "I know. You can even think yourself warm if you try—and I've tried."

"And it's really worked?"

"It helps. Sometimes when I was so cold over there that I could not sleep I would play a game with myself. I would say, 'Illi, you are not cold at all. You are lying beside a great big fire, you have ten blankets on you, and the whole place is cozy and warm as a barn full of cattle.' I would close my eyes and keep thinking, and

98

then I'd fall asleep. I could do it with the cold, but not when I was hungry."

Tom leaned on his broom and looked at her with interest, his sharp but kind eyes full of admiration. "This Army business begins to make sense when I hear stories like yours," he said soberly.

"I am glad to hear you say that, Tom. So many of the boys over here don't want to fight."

"Oh, I don't want to either, but somebody has to put a stop to things like you've been through; and if it's going to take fighting to do it, it's the young guys like me with nothing to lose who should do it."

"But you have something to lose. You had to give up your job pitching for the Waverly ball team, didn't you?"

Tom nodded. "Yeah, but it'll keep—I hope. When I come back—*if* I come back, I'll only be twenty-one, not too old to work up to a good team. And I ought to be in good shape. The Army's fine training."

He flexed his muscles like a strong man and struck a pose.

Illi laughed. She liked Tom better each time she saw him. She only wished Ardis would not take his devotion so casually.

"What are you aiming to do with yourself when you finish school, Illi?" he asked.

"I am not sure yet, but I think it will be to study fashion design. I seem to have a talent that way, Miss Patchin says."

"Well, you don't have to make up your mind yet," Tom said as he swatted a big spider. "You've still got another year at High."

"Yes," said Illi and then she remembered what had happened yesterday. "No, I have not. I shall tell you a secret, Tom. I have been promoted. I am a senior now."

"Well, well, how come?"

"It was my biography, my English paper. Miss Loudon was so pleased with it that she told the principal I should be doing senior work. It was only the English that held me back. So on Monday I go into the senior class. I have told no one yet."

"Why? Aren't you pleased about it?"

"Yes, of course, but—I hated to tell Ardis. It will worry her. She will be thinking that soon I may be off on my own business and she will be alone again."

"I don't think you need to worry about Ardis. She can take it. Besides she may be up and around by that time herself. Would you like me to tell her?"

"Oh, would you, Tom? It would be a big relief. Tell her I will not desert her, that I shall be right here . . ."

"Hold on there. I don't think I'd better say *that*."

"Why not?"

"Because you might not be. If I know the Enwrights, they won't let you tie yourself to Ardis. They'll want you to get ready for life just as if you were their own daughter. To tell the truth I think you're making a mountain out of a molehill. Why don't you just let things work themselves out? They often do."

"I suppose you are right," Illi said humbly and went to put Mark's room in order so they could use it as a dressing room.

It looked quite different now. There was a rag rug on the floor, a table desk, bookshelves, and a wardrobe to hold his clothes. She had painted that herself in dark, shiny black and decorated it with little stiff contorted figures engaged in various sports. She'd found a couch cover for his cot and had covered some old cushions with pieces of bright felt and corduroy. Mark and she had found a little potbellied stove in the attic and it kept the place as warm as toast. She had lettered a sign for his door; *The Lion's Den* she had called it because the lion was the symbol for St. Mark, and she had added a crouching lion with a book—as a reminder. Mark had been enthusiastic about his den and seemed quite content to spend his evenings there studying. She would often see his light still burning when she turned out her own at night.

Tom was rigging up the last electric bulb all ready for the pumpkin lanterns when Geegee and Mark came back with the decorations. Geegee was giggling as usual.

"We had such a time," she said. "First of all a bull chased us—"

"It wasn't a bull, it was only a cow," Mark said. "But you should have seen Geegee cover the ground to the fence. She looked like a ballet dancer being pursued by a faun."

"Then the jalopy broke down—"

"It didn't break down, Putty-Puss, it just had a loose connection," said Mark, resenting the slur against his car.

"Mark fixed it with one of my bobby pins," Geegee explained with one of her you-great-big-wonderful-man looks for Mark. "I think he's wonderful that way, don't you, Illi?"

"*Ja, er ist ein grossartiger Kerl—er hört sogar das Gras wachsen,*" she said with a sly look at Mark.

Mark laughed but Geegee pouted. "What did she say? I don't think it's polite, Illi, to talk a language other people don't know."

"Sometimes I do not understand your language," Illi reminded her.

"Never mind, Little One, we weren't talking about you. Illi was just telling you what a wonderful fellow I am—I can even hear the grass grow." He gave one of her curls a sharp yank. "In plain English how would you like to dance?" He went to put on a record but Illi stopped him.

"Not now. We have work to do. Save it for to-night."

Mark dropped the record and crouched as if Illi were holding a whip over him. "Yes, Excellency, no, Excellency, okay, Excellency," he whined. "Whatever you say."

"Then I say, go out and bring in the pumpkins so Tom can get to work on them."

"I do hope it's moonlight tonight," Geegee said dreamily.

"What difference does it make if the party's inside?" Tom asked.

"But it doesn't have to *stay* inside," Geegee said with a look at Mark who took her by the hand and led her to the door.

"Let's start with the sunshine," he said. "I need help. You can carry the pumpkins. I'm quite a boy with the corn."

They went off, Geegee still giggling, and Illi, leaving Tom to finish, went over to the house to see what she could do there, because she knew *Mütterchen* and

Daddy Bill were due at a dinner meeting of the Welfare Board that night.

The five of them were sitting around the dinner table when Neal rushed in. "I'd have been over earlier to help," he said, "but I had a job to do for the Major. Sick horse."

"Not Pokey?" Illi asked quickly.

"No, not Pokey. He sent his love to you, by the way. I think he misses you. Hasn't seen you all week."

Illi flushed as if Neal had been talking about a boy, or himself. "I've been busy," she said. "How's your German coming along?"

"Pretty good. It seems to make a little more sense now. Perhaps because I can hear you speaking it and it sounds more natural. I take that exam next week."

"You better let me give you a good—what do they say?—workout?"

At this they all laughed. Mark said, "You're learning fast, Illi."

"You'd be surprised how fast," Tom put in, a smile for Illi. "I'm going to tell them your news, shall I, Illi?" She gave him a short nod. "She's been promoted. She's a senior now. Isn't that fine?"

Illi threw a quick glance at Ardis who said in a hurt way, "Why, Illi! Why didn't you tell me?"

"She wanted to surprise you," Tom said quickly.

"And besides it isn't so very important, is it?" Illi asked. "Everything will be just the same."

"But it *is* important. We're all proud of you," Ardis said. "Aren't we, Mark? Neal?" as if they had not been duly excited.

"Of course." Neal came to thump Illi on the back. "Good for you, Illi. Now what?"

"Now what?" Illi repeated, her brows knit.

"I mean what will you be aiming for? College?"

"Must we talk about that now?" she asked, an anxious eye on Ardis.

But Ardis had wheeled her chair away from the table where they'd been sitting and was waiting for their attention. "I have some good news too," she said slowly. "The doctors think I may be able to get on my feet by Christmas. Of course it means braces but—" she gave an apologetic laugh, "it's a step forward, isn't it?"

"Oh, Ardis!" Illi ran and gave her a big hug. "That is the best news of all!"

Then everyone crowded round and shook her hand and Mark kissed her. It was clearly Ardis' night. Her cheeks burned with color, and when they wheeled her to the barn, which was lit with the grinning pumpkin faces Tom had made, it was like a triumphal procession, the boys ahead imitating trumpets with their hands before their mouths and the two girls following like two faithful handmaids.

Illi thought, if it could just stay like this without the Prentices to spoil it. She hoped they wouldn't come. But

they did, Peachy looking like a cute dancing doll with her wide skirt of quilted sateen, Phil like a pale, unhappy stork standing first on one foot and then the other behind Ardis' chair.

Mark put a stack of records on the player and started the dancing, swinging Geegee out onto the floor. Neal and Peachy followed them. Tom and Illi and Phil stood beside Ardis until Tom said to Phil, "Why don't you and Illi dance? I'll sit it out with Ardis. She's my girl tonight."

But Phil shook his head. "I don't dance much," he said. "You go ahead."

"Yes, you two dance," Ardis insisted.

And so Illi danced with Tom. "I am afraid I am not much of a dancer either," she said. "I have never had much chance to dance like this. You should see me do the *czardas* though."

"Show me," said Tom.

"Here?"

"Why not?"

"We need some lively music. Later I'll find a record that will do."

They danced in silence until Tom said, "I hate to leave Ardis with that drip. He doesn't seem to have a word to say."

Illi looked back to where Phil still stood beside Ardis, saying nothing. "I'll get rid of him," she said.

"Would you? Then I can cut in on Peachy and—"

"And Neal can keep Ardis company," Illi laughed. "That is what you meant, isn't it?"

With a little tact she managed to steer the bored boy

to a corner and the subject to books. He came alive then and kept the conversational ball rolling.

"They say I read too much," he told Illi. "But I don't think so. I get more out of books than I do out of people."

"But you should remember that it is people who make the books, people write them and they have to know all about other people to do it."

Phil looked at her with his nearsighted eyes. "You know, you have something there," he said. "I never thought of it that way. Do you like books?"

Illi said she did. Then she had a fine idea. "How would you like to see Mr. Enwright's? I'll take you over to his study if he's still out."

The study was empty. Phil stood looking at the shelves like a little boy in a candy shop. He put up his hand to pull out a few of the books but Illi stopped him. "No, no, must not touch," she said with a laugh.

"But I wouldn't hurt them," he said surprised.

"Of course not, but Mr. Enwright is very particular who handles them. I never have, but I am going to catalogue them for him shortly."

"You are? I wish I could help you. Do you think he would let me?" he asked wistfully.

Illi hesitated. "I don't know. But I can ask him. He might. He is very particular though, especially about his first editions. Those shelves there are all firsts."

"I can see that," Phil said. "I've started to collect in a small way. Well, standing here is only a temptation. Let's go back to the party. If you can put up with me I'd like to dance with you."

But when they went back to the barn there was no

party, only Tom bending over Ardis' chair and Illi could have sworn she was crying.

"I guess the moonlight was too much for them," Tom said with a worried look at Illi.

"That's Peachy for you," Phil said with disgust. "She'll do it every time. I don't know what she goes to parties for."

"Well, she won't do it here," Illi said fiercely and went outside to look for the others. She found Mark just about to start up the jalopy and Geegee with him.

"Where are you going?" she asked in an icy voice.

"Just for a little air. It was hot in there—"

"It was not hot," she said. "I am ashamed of you, Mark. To walk out on Ardis this way. Have you no feelings for her at all? This is her first party for years and you go off and leave her alone."

"She wasn't alone. Tom was with her."

"One man does not make a party. If I were you, I would go in there and start the music again. And as for you, Geegee Fairchild, I am ashamed of you, too. I thought you had better manners."

She heard Mark mutter something and Geegee laugh and whisper "Mrs. Gestapo in person," but she did not care. She went off looking for Neal and Peachy. It was then she realized the Prentice car was gone, and knew Neal and Peachy had gone off together. And now she was really angry and hurt and disappointed. She would not have believed that Neal would do a thing like this, not when he knew how much the party meant to Ardis. Of course she knew Peachy had a hand in it, but Neal should have been able to stand on his own two feet and keep things in hand.

It was almost an hour later when Peachy and Neal turned up. The six of them in the barn had tried to keep up the appearance of a party. Mark had been very gay, and Geegee had got over her sulks. She had even danced with Phil, who wasn't so bad after all, and they had organized a sort of Paul Jones with Ardis' chair in the ring. But it had not been a good party. Everyone was trying too hard.

"Well," Tom said when he caught sight of the two truants, "where have you two been? Coon hunting?"

Peachy gave him a smile and came over to Ardis to say in a pretty, apologetic way, "I'm sorry we were so long. We were only going to be a few minutes but—well, Neal found something to do, and I had to wait with him." She threw a smile at Neal who frowned and looked thoroughly uncomfortable.

When the music started Mark took Peachy away and Phil danced off with Geegee. It left Neal and Illi looking at each other, and in a moment she was in his arms, moving in time to the music.

"I would not be dancing with you except that I want to talk to you," she said angrily.

"And I to you," he replied. "I want to explain things, Illi . . ."

"Do not bother," she cut him off. "It is Ardis to whom you should apologize. It was an unkind trick to go off like that and break things up."

"It was no trick. I was worried about something and Peachy got the idea—"

"Of course. 'The woman tempted me and I did bite of the apple,' " she said disgustedly. "Now I must go over to the house. You had better go and amuse Ardis and make your peace with her."

"But she has Tom," he said. "He's the one that counts."

"With Ardis?" she asked in surprise.

"Haven't you noticed? Anyone can see he worships the ground she—I was about to say walks on, but that isn't so good. He worships the air she breathes. All he wants is to see her happy."

"Then he ought to have it in for you for making her unhappy."

"Me? How could I?"

"You did tonight. She was crying when Peachy and you went off and stayed."

Neal looked troubled. "She needn't have. Peachy means nothing to me. No girl means that much to me—I mean, look Illi, we've got to talk this thing out."

"Some other time," she said coolly. "I have to go help Mrs. Grimm with the sandwiches."

"I'll go, too."

"No, you stay here. And Neal, please be nice to Ardis. I think you started something that night when you called her Princess and now you'll have to finish it somehow."

When she came back with the sandwiches the party was in full swing again. They were deep in Halloween fortunes. Ardis' apple paring had turned into an *N* when she threw it over her shoulder, Geegee was trying desperately to make an *M* out of the hot lead she was dropping into cold water, and Peachy and Tom were bobbing for apples. Phil was deep in the book of charms Ardis had found.

Everything was fine and Ardis seemed to be enjoying herself. That was all that mattered. Time enough to think of what was going on in Illi's own mixed-up mind. That could wait.

Chapter 10

IT WAS THANKSGIVING before Illi got around to working on Mr. Enwright's books. It had been a busy and mixed-up time. Neal had submitted to her hard, relentless coaching to pass his German test, which he did with a good mark. She had also given Mark a lift with his French. Tom went back to camp, his long leave over. And she had settled down into the old routine with Ardis, introducing her to the new studies she was being given in the senior classes. Once she went to a football game with Mark when Geegee couldn't go and enjoyed it. But, for the most part, she spent her Saturdays at home.

There had been a few rides with Neal on the good

days, but it was not the way it had been at first. Neal seemed stiff and uncomfortable with her; and if it had not been for seeing Pokey, she would have preferred not to ride at all. When he came over in the evenings she made a point of leaving him alone with Ardis and went to her room to study or sew. She would hear them downstairs playing Ardis' records or chattering over a game of checkers or anagrams and she tried to fight down the jealousy that stirred within her. It would not have been so bad if it had been Peachy, because then she could have been honestly jealous and not ashamed of it. But with Ardis—all she hoped was that Neal would not hurt her. Because Ardis was acting more and more as if Neal belonged to her and Illi felt sure Neal belonged to nobody at this point. He had to keep himself free and ready to tackle the big job that lay before him.

Then one day they were invited to the Prentices' for an after-the-game tea dance. Ardis was excited. It was the first party she had been asked to attend since she'd been doomed to her wheel chair and she dressed for it as carefully as if she were not going to be wheeled in, her legs and ankles useless.

Illi helped her with her hair and lifted the lovely bronzy-brown dress of whispering taffeta over her head. It was scoop-necked and almost sleeveless and it set off Ardis' creamy skin to perfection. Her summer freckles were almost gone and as Illi stood off to admire her she thought that Ardis was becoming a really beautiful girl.

"Do you know you have the most beautiful neck and arms?" she told her.

"Have I?" Ardis wheeled herself over to her mirror.

"Well, I'm thankful for that much. And some day my legs will be just as nice. That will be the day, Illi."

"Yes," said Illi, "that will be the day." But her heart was aching because she knew it was still a long way off. The doctors had said Ardis was making progress, that they hoped to get her into braces by Christmas and teach her to walk again. But that would be a long process. The main thing, they said, was to keep her happy and hopeful, to see that she led a normal life and to treat her as if she were no different from any other seventeen-year-old girl. So now they were going to a party together and what could be more normal for two girls in their teens?

"I suppose there will be a lot of strangers there," Ardis said thoughtfully. "I hope I won't get stage fright. You'll help me, won't you, Illi? And Neal will, too, if he's there."

"Oh, he will be there," Illi said. "Peachy will not overlook Neal, you can be sure."

Ardis looked at her queerly. "You said that in such a funny way. What did you mean?"

"I meant that Peachy thinks she has put her mark on Neal."

"And has she?" Ardis asked in a small, weak voice.

"I doubt it. I do not think Neal is ready to let any girl mark him for her own, or to go steady with anyone. Neal knows he has a big job ahead. If he does get appointed to West Point—"

"West Point? That's news to me."

"Oh! I thought you knew," Illi said. "The way your mother talked I thought the Major had told her. Well, it's out now, but please don't tell Neal I told you. The thing I wanted to say is that it means four full years for Neal before he can think of getting married. And four years is a long time for any girl to wait."

"Not for a girl like me," Ardis said, "that's the best thing I do, wait." There were tears in her voice. "Oh, I know what you are trying to do, Illi. You're trying to warn me about Neal. But please, please, let me dream. I haven't much of anything else to dream about, have I?"

"Ardis, Ardis darling!" Illi was down on her knees beside her. "I was not trying to warn you against Neal. I like him, too. But I do not want to see you hurt. You are so—so honest about how you feel, your heart is on your sleeve. And I am afraid of what Peachy might try to do today. She was not very nice here at your party."

"Oh, Neal told me all about that," Ardis said. "They just drove over to see that sick horse and then the Major asked him to wait until the vet got there for instructions."

"Well, maybe that is the way it was, but—watch Peachy."

"Forewarned is forearmed," Ardis tried to laugh. "I see where I shall have to be charming and gay and forget I am just half a girl in a wheel chair—no competition at all."

Mark was to drive them over in the Enwright station wagon. "Take it slow," Mr. Enwright said as he and Mark pushed Ardis up the ramp of boards into the back and fastened the clamps that would keep her chair from rolling. It was his own device to make her riding easier and he was very proud of it.

"Don't worry. Illi won't let me drive too fast," Mark said with a wry face for Illi.

"And be very careful getting her out," Mr. Enwright cautioned.

"Oh, Daddy, I'm not made of glass," Ardis said, and as they drove off, "Well, it won't be like this always."

"No, next year you'll be dancing," said Mark and Illi wondered if he really believed it.

It was a big party, but even so the huge room was not crowded. Illi stuck close to Ardis' chair to help her over the hard spots while Mark went off to bring back the people he knew to meet her. But she need not have worried about Ardis. Never had Illi seen her so gay, so unconcerned with her inability to join the fun, so eager to meet new people. She introduced Illi as "My sister, the clever one of the family, you know." It made Illi's heart sing with gratitude as well as admiration.

Even when the dancing began Ardis was never alone. Once when Illi left her to dance with Mark she came back to find a group around the chair convulsed with laughter at Ardis' stories. "You should see them getting me into that pool," she was saying, "just like a tadpole. on a long stick. And when they get me into the car it's like moving a baby grand piano."

"Okay," said one boy, jumping to his feet, "how about making like a merry-go-round?" And he grabbed her chair and wheeled her off among the dancers who cut in one after another until Illi was afraid Ardis would be dizzy.

"Quite a girl, isn't she?" Illi heard someone beside her saying and she turned to see Phil Prentice beside her. "Look, before someone comes up and asks you to dance I wish you'd come with me. I have something to show you."

She let him lead her from the big living room across the hall to a smaller one, a library much larger than Mr. Enwright's but just as full of books. They were neat books in sets, many of them stacked on shelves behind glass doors. She wondered if they were ever read. Then Phil went to a closet that was part of the paneling and opened it.

"This is mine," he said. "Mother makes me keep my books here because she says they are too shabby to look at, but I've picked up quite a few good ones. Take this copy of *Alice in Wonderland*, good condition, dated." He lifted it from the shelf for Illi to examine. "Cost me plenty. I've paid as high as fifty dollars for a book."

"Fifty dollars! Your hobby must be an expensive luxury," Illi said, holding the book gingerly. "Does your father give you the money to buy these books?"

A shadow passed over the boy's face. "No, he doesn't," he said resentfully. "If it was a horse I wanted, he'd pass out the money and he wouldn't say a word. But books—he just can't understand anyone paying that for old ones. He thinks it's sissy."

"Then how do you get the money?"

His eyes shifted uneasily. "I save it up," he said and took the book away from her and closed the closet door. "By the way, I thought you were going to let me help you with Mr. Enwright's books."

"I haven't started on them yet."

"When you do, can I help? Will you ask him?"

Illi said she would and was starting to leave the room when Peachy appeared in the doorway.

"Oh," she said, "I wondered who was in here. I'm looking for Neal. Has anyone seen him?"

"No. Is he coming?" Illi asked with politeness.

Peachy knit her brows. "I'm waiting for him to help me with the motion-picture machine. We got some dandy pictures at the Pimlico races last week."

"We! She means Dad and she, not Neal," Phil said, winking at Illi.

"Oh, I knew that," Illi said easily, "because Neal was at our house then. Ardis and he watched the whole thing on the TV set."

Peachy gave her a cold stare and Phil laughed out loud.

"That for you, Sis! Other people like horses, too, you know."

"Well, they're better than a lot of dusty old books that aren't worth shelf space." She turned to Illi. "How is Pokey by the way, or don't you know?"

"Oh, I know. He's fine. Shall I tell him you were asking for him?"

"Yes. Tell him Dad has a deal on with the Major and maybe he'll soon be moving over to our stables."

Illi stood like a statue watching Peachy flounce out the door. It couldn't be true, it couldn't. She felt as if she were standing before a judge who had just handed out a sentence. She wet her lips and turned to Phil.

"Is it true?" she asked him in a voice that was like a croak.

Phil shrugged. "Probably. I know Dad has a horse the Major wants and maybe they've made some kind of a swap. Trust Peachy to get what she wants especially if it's a horse—or a man."

Chapter 11

MARK DROVE THEM home early from the Prentice party and then after helping Illi to wheel Ardis into the house went back to finish the evening. Neal had not put in an appearance when they said good-by to the Prentices and she could see that Ardis was worrying about it. The bright little balloon that was flying so high at the party had begun to deflate on the way home.

"What do you suppose happened to Neal?" she asked Illi, who was helping her get ready for bed. "He never disappoints people like that."

"Would you like me to call him?"

"Oh no! Maybe he'll ride over tomorrow if it's a nice day and we'll find out then."

But Sunday was a nice day and there was no sign of Neal. Late in the afternoon Illi announced she was going for a walk.

"Where to?" Ardis demanded suspiciously.

"I thought I might go over to the Major's."

"To see Neal?"

"No, to see the Major."

"But whatever for?"

"Because I've got to see him about Pokey right away." Illi's voice held the alarm she had been trying to fight down ever since the scene with Peachy in the Prentice library. "Peachy says her father is going to buy him for her, and the Major promised me he wasn't going to sell Pokey to anyone right away."

Ardis knit her brows. "But, Illi, you can't expect the Major to keep a horse just for your use."

"No, but—oh, Ardis, if you knew what that horse means to me! I have felt like a different person since I came to know Pokey. He seems to belong to me. I think it may be because he too has Hungarian heritage."

"Hungarian? How could that be?"

Illi told her the story of the contraband horses and her suspicions that Pokey might very well be the foal of one of the horses she had known, perhaps even of Vidám. "He looks so much like Vidám that it is not coincidence. If I could only get down to that place in Maryland and see for myself," she sighed.

"But how could you know? Could you recognize a horse after so many years—how many is it?"

"Only eight. I'd know. I'd know Vidám anywhere."

"But what good would it do you, Illi? You couldn't

hope to own such a horse and I'm sure Daddy couldn't afford to buy him for you."

"I don't expect that for a minute. But it would be so wonderful to meet him. It would be like seeing an old friend from home, almost as good as finding Janni again."

Ardis' eyes softened. "Well, don't worry yet. Maybe Peachy was wrong about Pokey. I think she exaggerates to fit the occasion, don't you?"

"Yes, but she doesn't like me. She's jealous."

"Jealous? Of you?"

"Well, you see I am the one she has met with Neal most of the time. She started showing me how she felt the very first time we went over there."

"I see." Ardis looked off beyond her window toward the Wallace pastures that still showed green in the distance. Her eyes were troubled. "But I don't understand why a nice girl like Peachy would be so—so nasty."

"I think she is spoiled by her father perhaps. She always gets what she wants, even her own brother says that, and she wants Pokey because she knows I want him, too. I have just got to get him, somehow."

"But, Illi, how can you? He must be worth a lot. The Major doesn't bother with horses that can be bought for a song."

"I know. But the Major said he would not sell him to anyone right away and I have been hoping that I could make some money in some way to buy him myself. There must be some way to do it. Everyone in America seems to be able to make money."

Ardis studied her, a frown on her forehead. "When

you set mind to something, you keep it set, don't you, Illi?"

"Yes. I have had to," Illi said with tight lips. "It is the only way I have been able to get along. Over there I made up my mind I was going to get to America somehow—and I did."

"And now that you're here, are you sorry?"

"No, you know I am not. But . . ."

"But what?"

"It is all so different. I can act like an American but I cannot think like one. I—I still feel as if I did not belong."

"Oh, Illi, darling, how can you say that? When we've all tried to make you feel at home, when all we want is to see you happy?" Ardis was genuinely distressed.

Illi went to lay her cheek against Ardis' and said with unaccustomed emotion, "Please, please do not misunderstand me. I am not unhappy, but always when I begin to feel that things are right, something happens. It has always been that way. Maybe I talk this way now because of all the talk about these 'wild horses.' It made me think again of the old times. It is like seeing a face from home in a crowd and it passes on before you can speak to it and you are alone again."

"I wish I had a lot of money, I'd buy Pokey for you," Ardis said impulsively. "But I have no money. What would I do with it?"

"I would not take your money, Ardis, but I do love you for thinking of it. Now I shall go and talk to the Major. There may be something I can do. He seemed very kind and understanding when we talked about Pokey before. Good-by. I will not be long."

"If you see Neal . . ."

"I'll give him your love," Illi said with a laugh and was off.

It was a lovely day, the trees still holding on to the last colors of autumn. The walk over to the Wallace place would have been a pleasant one if it had not been for the nature of her errand. She was not sure yet what she was going to say to the Major, but she had not come wholly unprepared. In her pocket was her purse and in the purse were her savings, almost fifty dollars. The Enwrights had given her a generous allowance from the first week she had come. "This is to take care of your clothes and your weekly expenses with a little over for a good time," Mr. Enwright had said. Then he had seen the shadow of embarrassment on her face and he had added quickly, "It is *not* a salary, Illi, though I am sure you will more than earn it. It is what most American fathers do for their daughters—so you won't be pestering us for money all the time." He laughed. Then he spoke soberly again. "We want you to be independent and the first and easiest way is to have your own money to spend."

But she had spent very little of it. She had so few needs, no clothes as yet, for Mrs. Enwright had outfitted her well when she first came and had given her permission to dig into the big chest of materials for anything she wanted to make. Bus fare, lunches, and school supplies took very little and she had been able to put away over half her allowance every week. She kept it in a tin box in her room and gloated over it like a young miser.

But now she had taken it all for Pokey. Of course she knew she did not have enough to buy a horse, but maybe she could put—as they called it over here—a down payment on him and make some arrangement with the Major to pay the rest in installments, just as Mark had planned to buy his fancy car. Maybe the Major might let her work off the rest of the money. She could work in the stables as well as any man, or she could take that job in the dress shop if Mrs. Enwright would let her.

She walked up the drive to the Wallace house, her fingers crossed in the pockets of her coat. She had never been in the house, only to the stables with Neal. Her heart was thumping as she lifted the knocker on the big white door.

It was opened by a pleasant-faced woman and immediately Illi knew it was Neal's mother. They looked exactly alike, the same hazel eyes, the same warm smile.

"I've come to see Major Wallace," she said. "I'm Illi Horvath. Is he home?"

"No, he isn't, but come in!" Mrs. Austin held the door wide and Illi with a polite thank you went into the wide hall that divided the house from front to back. It was white paneled and filled with things from all over the world probably brought back by the Major from his travels. There were teakwood chests and bolo knives and carved screens and Fiji masks, all looking queer in the plain Colonial setting.

"The Major and Neal are both away," Mrs. Austin was saying, "but I would be so happy if you would stay and talk to me, perhaps let me give you a cup of tea or hot chocolate. I'm Neal's mother, you know. He's told me so much about you girls."

She led the way through the hall to a wing at the back. Here there was a small sitting room, cozy and warm, a fire on the hearth and the radio going merrily.

"These are our quarters," Mrs. Austin said. "Please

make yourself comfortable. And tell me, is there anything I can do for you while the Major is away?"

"No-o," Illi said, "I think not. It was about the horse
—Pokey, the one Mr. Prentice is supposed to be buying."

Mrs. Austin shook her head. "I'm afraid I don't know
much about that end of the place," she said. "My job
here is to keep the Major comfortable—and Neal's nose
in his books." She gave a light laugh. "Neal does like a
good time. But he's beginning to realize he has to work
to get what he wants out of life. And do you know something? I think you have helped to change his attitude."

"I?" Illi asked in surprise. "How?"

"Well, he admires you tremendously and keeps telling me of all the things you had to fight and rise above."

"But what about Ardis? She is the one who should in-
spire him."

"Oh, she does. There's no doubt of that. She must be
a brave girl, but . . ." she dropped her voice as if she
were telling a secret and there was a mischievous note in
her voice, "I think he feels more at home with you. You
speak the same language."

Illi laughed. "Well, it is not German, I assure you. I
feel comfortable with Neal, too," she confided. Then
she said, "May I ask how soon the Major will be home?"

"Tonight, or perhaps not until tomorrow morning.
He went down to Maryland yesterday on business and
he took Neal along to drive for him. A long drive like
that tires him."

"To Maryland? Where Pokey came from?"

"That I don't know, but he has a friend who has a
stock farm down there. He raises horses."

"Oh dear, if I had only known!" Illi said ruefully. "I

would have hid myself in the trunk so I could have gone along. I would so much like to see the horses that produced Pokey."

"You seem to love that horse very much."

"I do, I do. Look, Mrs. Austin, could you—would you mind asking the Major not to do anything about Pokey until I can see him and talk to him? I brought a little money with me, only forty-nine dollars, but I have a business proposition to put to him. I think I should die if Peachy Prentice gets that horse."

"Oh, so Peachy is in this, is she?" A cold look came into Mrs. Austin's eyes. "She's a nice girl but I wish she would leave Neal alone. She keeps calling and calling and I have to make excuses for him. Why can't girls have more pride?"

Illi smiled. "That is one thing I have felt lacking in the American girls and boys I have met—pride. But perhaps I have too much. Will you speak to the Major, please, Mrs. Austin?"

"I think it would be better if I asked Neal to do it. He will know more about the whole thing, and I believe you can trust Neal to put in a good word for you if it is necessary. Now shall we have some hot chocolate and some of my almond tarts? I'm very proud of them. Neal says you can cook, too, and that you are a wonderful seamstress. Would you like to come into the kitchen with me?"

An hour later Illi left the Wallace house, carrying with her a box of the tarts for Ardis. She had enjoyed her visit with Mrs. Austin so much. It was pure woman-talk, no problems, just clothes, recipes, movies, and radio. As she walked home slowly through the fall dusk she lost the tenseness and the fear that had accompanied her on the way over to the Major's. She knew part of her good mood was due to the comfortable, assuring manner of Mrs. Austin, the same thing she always felt in Neal. Where either of them was, the world would be a better place to live in, perhaps because they felt that everyone was essentially good and refused to distrust anyone. She wished she could be like that. But she did trust Neal, and part of her good feeling was the knowledge that Neal would do his best to keep the Major from acting upon Pokey right away. Like the little Dutch boy she had a finger in the dyke. It remained to be seen how long she could hold back the flood.

Chapter 12

"PHIL PRENTICE HAS been calling you like mad," Ardis told her when she got home. "What did you do to him, Illi? Bewitch him?"

"No, no. He is not interested in me. He is interested only in his books. Is Daddy Bill home?"

"Yes, I think he's in the study. Did you see Neal?"

"No. He and Major Wallace were both away. They drove to Maryland yesterday."

"Oh." Ardis said it with relief. "That explains it. I didn't think Neal would let Peachy down with no explanation at all. I bet she knew where he was all the time."

"Could be," said Illi, grinning with pride at the expression she had just picked up. "Maybe Peachy did not believe him when he said he was going to Maryland and she wanted to see what we would say."

"Maybe. Do you suppose their trip had anything to do with Pokey?"

"I have no idea. Mrs. Austin did not know either. She is a very pleasant woman, Ardis. She says we, you and I, have both made a new man out of Neal." Illi laughed. "And something else," she dropped her voice to a whisper, "I do not think she approves of Peachy Prentice at all."

"Hurray for Mrs. Austin! Look, Illi, there is something I want to say to you about Neal. I do like him very much as you know, but I've been thinking about what you said, about his not wanting to stick to one girl right now. I think that's true. So I want you to know that I am not going to be silly about a boy who is not crazy over me."

Illi's eyes blurred with tears. Ardis was trying to be brave about Neal, knowing she could not compete with girls like Peachy or even herself. She wondered if perhaps Ardis were trying to withdraw in her favor. Her heart ached to be able to tell Ardis she was wrong, that Neal *was* crazy about her. But she knew it wouldn't be so. Neal was crazy about nobody. She said, as casually as she could, as if it were not important, "So, the dream is over?"

"Yes, this dream is over. And don't think I feel badly about it, because I don't. You see, I haven't had much experience with boys and I have to learn how to take them. That's all."

"Maybe you'll soon have a new dream," Illi suggested.

"A new dream? About whom? Who could it be?"

"It could be Tom Grimm."

"Tom?" Ardis' eyes were wide with surprise. "But I've known him such a long time, ever since we came here. He's been awfully sweet to me but I've never thought of him that way."

"Well, you would not be silly to dream about Tom Grimm because *he* is crazy over you."

"He is? How do you know?"

"By the way he talks about you and looks at you. Everyone can see it but you, Ardis."

"But I've thought he was just sorry for me . . ."

"Oh no. Tom is not sorry for you. He knows there is nothing to be sorry about. He says you can take anything and that you will soon be walking around like anyone else."

"Did he really say that?" A soft red came flowing into her round cheeks and her eyes were like two stars. "It's good to be liked for oneself, not for one's misfortunes," she said softly. "I think I shall write to Tom tonight, tell him we're hoping he can get home for Thanksgiving."

Illi brought her writing paper and pen and went off to speak to Mr. Enwright about Phil. She didn't really want to bother Daddy Bill and she would rather have tackled the job of putting his books in order by herself, but she did feel sorry for Phil Prentice and she had promised him she would ask if he could work with her. Nobody in the big Prentice house seemed to care about Phil's hobby to which he had as much right as they had to their horses. Between a good horse and a good book it might be a toss-up. Both could be good friends.

Mr. Enwright looked up from his book when she tapped on his open door. "Hello, Bright Eyes! Where have you been all day?"

"I went to see a man about a horse," Illi said with a grin.

"Ah! Did you get him?"

"No, not yet. Listen, Daddy Bill, would you consider letting someone help me with this job of putting your books in order?"

"Depends on who it is. Are you getting cold feet?"

"Oh no. But there's a boy, Phil Prentice—"

"Oh yes, Clem Prentice's boy. What's he like? Clem speaks as if his son were rather hopeless."

"Just quiet and likes books better than horses."

"That's no sin. So he wants to help you?"

"Yes. He was interested in your books. I didn't let him touch a thing," she assured him.

"Well," Mr. Enwright seemed to be considering this seriously, "I don't like to think of strangers handling my books; some of them are quite valuable as I've pointed out to you. But if you are willing to take the responsibility—"

"I would expect to do that," Illi said.

"And if you don't let him mess around in here when you're not here, I'll say yes. When do you expect to start?"

"This week, I hope. I thought we could get a lot done during the Thanksgiving vacation. I'm going to get a little box and some cards—"

"I'll bring a regular file home from town tomorrow. I'm interested to know how you're going to go about this thing. I wouldn't know where to start. And I hope you're not going to put me out in the barn while you do it."

Illi laughed. "No fear. I have it all planned. I will do a little bit at a time when you are not here. You will never know what is going on."

"Fine. You know, Illi, you have an enviable quality that many women do not have, the ability of making a man feel very comfortable. You seem to delight in taking care of us all. I've watched you with Mark. Hold on to it."

"Perhaps it is the Old World in me," Illi grinned. "Over there that is a woman's first job."

"Well, it should pay off," Mr. Enwright laughed. "The men should come flocking around here like flies around honey." He looked up at his cluttered shelves. "It will be a treat to walk over there and put my finger on a book instead of spending a whole evening looking for it."

But it was another week before Illi could get to work. Neal had asked her to his Thanksgiving prom at the Academy and she was busy making a formal for herself. She had found a length of lovely glazed chintz in Mrs. Enwright's box, material bought for curtains and rejected. It was a beautiful shade of blue, exactly the china blue of Illi's eyes, and there was plenty of it. Illi cut the skirt so it would billow properly and fitted the bodice tight, scalloping both the bodice top and the bottom of the skirt and binding them with more chintz in a deep rose color. From top and bottom peeped ruffles of pleated net and right at the front of the bodice was a rose that never bloomed on any bush, a modern thing of rose chintz petals bound with the blue arising from a center made from a rhinestone button Mrs. Enwright had given her.

"It looks like a Dior creation," Ardis had said enthusiastically when Illi tried on the finished dress in front of Ardis' long mirror.

"It's clever, very clever, Illi," Mrs. Enwright had said. "You have a fine fashion sense. Would you like to study fashion design?"

"I have been thinking of it," Illi told her. "Miss Patchin thinks I might get a scholarship somewhere. But —" But she didn't tell them that she must get to work and make some money so she could buy Pokey. Neal had assured her that there was nothing in the rumor that the Major was going to sell Pokey to Mr. Prentice. But when she had asked him about the Maryland trip he would say nothing except that the Major had gone there on business.

"I rather thought Peachy was just doing some wishful thinking," she told Neal.

"Peachy thinks because she wants a thing to be so, it will be," he said. "She has a lot to learn."

"Will she be at this dance?"

"Probably. She knows a lot of Academy boys. Phil goes there too, you know."

It was probably the prospect of meeting Peachy rather than Neal's approval that had set her sewing furiously on her "Dior creation." Another thing that disturbed her was the fact that Ardis could not go to the dance. It had given her a guilty feeling. Ardis had been wonderful about it, but once Illi had come in to find her in tears. She wished then she had said no to Neal, and she even called him at the last minute and suggested he ask someone else, even Peachy, if it were not too late. But Neal had refused.

"Illi, you've got to be sensible about Ardis. Just staying home with her isn't going to help. Then she'd feel doubly bad. Besides she won't be alone. Isn't Grimm supposed to be home for Thanksgiving? I'm sure if he is, he'll spend it with Ardis."

"I hope so, because Mark won't be home that night either. He's taking Geegee to his freshman prom over at Bartram."

So she had given in and gone to the dance with Neal and she had had a wonderful time. Peachy had given them both the cold shoulder, which was a relief, and plenty of boys had cut in on Neal so she was never alone for a minute. In the dressing room she had caught the

swift, curious glances of the other girls, none of whom was better dressed than she but all of whom were wearing far more expensive dresses.

One bubbling little girl, more honest than the rest, put the question bluntly: "I adore your dress. Where did you get it? I've never seen anything quite like it. Is it an imported model?"

"No," Illi said with secret amusement, "but it was made by a foreign designer."

"Oh! I thought I recognized the French touch," she said nodding her head knowingly. "Those French, they can do wonders with anything, even mosquito netting."

Mosquito netting! There was an idea. She might try that, too, sometime. The experience left her feeling more sure of herself than she had been since her arrival in America.

It was at the dance that she made the first date with Phil to start on the books. "We can begin tomorrow," she told him. "The Enwrights are going away for the week end. We should make good progress."

So they had holed in in Mr. Enwright's study while Tom entertained Ardis. He was teaching her a new card game he had learned in the recreation hall in camp. From the study she could hear Ardis' fresh laughter and Tom's rumbling chuckle. They were having a good time and Illi was glad of it.

Her plan was to call off the titles and authors of the books and let Phil type the cards. It was slow work because Phil would insist on dipping into the pages of a book and get lost in it, but they did make progress. Soon the cards piled up and Illi planned to take them to her room to arrange at night so she would not disturb Mr. Enwright.

"When I get the cards all arranged as I think they should be," she told Phil, "we can tackle the books, a shelf at a time." But it took some time before this point was reached. Sometimes Ardis would wheel herself in to watch them and help when she could.

She was there the day Phil said, "Some day I shall have a collection like this. I intend to go in for book collecting in a big way when I get my hands on my own money. I have some coming to me from my Grandmother Prentice when I'm of age."

"You and your books are as bad as Illi and her horses," Ardis said with a smile for Illi.

"Yes, but I have no Grandmother Prentice," Illi laughed. "I'll have to wait until I can make my own money."

Phil looked around the book-lined room. "They both cost a lot," he said, "old books and good horses."

"That's right," Illi agreed, picking up a book from the shelf of Mr. Enwright's treasures. "Take this copy of Hawthorne's *Scarlet Letter*. This one alone would buy a good horse." She turned the pages thoughtfully as if weighing its worth.

"Would it really?" Ardis seemed surprised. "I didn't know it was old enough for that."

"Well, it's not only a first edition but it has a long, personal, and important inscription written by the author—see?" She handed the book to them to study. "That makes it valuable because there is only one of it."

"Wonderful," Phil said, awe in his voice. "What's it worth?"

Illi knew because she had seen the details of its history in Mr. Enwright's little red book where he kept a record of his purchases and sales, but she did not feel it was something she could tell. "I can't tell you exactly," she said, "but it cost plenty, more than you or I could afford, Phil."

"Oh!" said Phil and handed it back to her with reverence.

The work went on for several weeks, Illi working on the cards at night, and she and Phil together when Mr. Enwright was not using the study. Perched on a ladder, she would call for the books and Phil would find them and hand them to her to be arranged according to the cards. A week before Christmas it was finished and Illi felt a real glow of satisfaction when she looked at the neat room.

Mr. Enwright was delighted. He acted like a small boy with a new bike, going through the shelves and pulling out books here and there. "Now," he said, "I can go out and buy a lot of new books. I have room for them."

"Oh, please!" Illi cried. "Not just yet. Not until you get used to finding things here. And please, Daddy Bill, don't try to put a book back when you have finished with it. Just leave it on the desk as they do in the library and I'll take care of it."

"I see you don't trust me," he said. "Well, I don't blame you. I promise I'll be good and not get the place in disorder again."

They went into the living room together to announce that everything was finished in the study.

"Well, I must say I'm glad," Ardis said. "Not only for Daddy's sake but for my own. I haven't seen anything of you lately, Illi. Neither has Neal. He's been complaining about it. I think he was really hurt yesterday when you refused to go riding with him."

"I couldn't help it. I had to work quickly while Daddy Bill was away. Did he say anything about Pokey?"

"Oh, Pokey's still there in Major Wallace's stables."

"I know. Neal says the Major isn't selling him."

Mr. Enwright seemed interested. "What makes this Pokey such a wonder horse, Illi? What could the Major get for him?"

"I have no idea. He was a gift to the Major and he has no papers. Even though he's probably a thoroughbred he can only be called a half-bred. So I'm hoping he isn't worth too much. I have my fingers crossed that the Major won't sell him until I can save up enough to buy him."

"Well, I'd say you were ambitious." Mr. Enwright laughed.

"She has faith and determination," said Ardis with a swift look at her father. "Perhaps you'll be rewarded, Illi. Perhaps Santa Claus will put him in your stocking for Christmas."

Illi let out a hoot of disbelief. "I believe there is a Santa Claus," she said, "but that would be a miracle beyond his power."

"But miracles still happen," Ardis said softly. "If I get my braces for Christmas that will be a miracle, too."

Chapter 13

*T*HE WEEK BEFORE Christmas was a busy one. Illi had never seen such preparations. Lists were prepared, and everyone kept going off into corners with everybody else to consult in mysterious whispers. The Saturday before the big day Mark surprised her by offering to drive her into the city to do her shopping.

"It's six for you and a half-dozen for himself," Ardis chuckled. "He wants you to help him with his own shopping."

"Well, what of it?" Mark defended himself. "Illi will profit by it. I shall provide the transportation and a good lunch."

Illi agreed and they started off early. The city was crowded, and Mark had a hard time finding a place to park. "Meet me for lunch," he said, "at the Crescent. I have to get some cash first anyway."

And so Illi had spent the rest of the morning on her own shopping and the afternoon on Mark's. They came home through the first snowstorm, the back seat of the jalopy filled with their packages. The country was already white as they came up the drive, and the lighted house set against the white hill looked warm and cozy and safe, and Illi could hardly wait to get inside. "Why, it is really coming home," she thought as she sniffed the odor of fresh cookies in the hall.

Ardis was waiting to hear about their day and full of the story of her own experiences. She had been down in the kitchen all day helping her Mother and Mrs. Grimm, shredding almonds, sugaring cookies, and so on.

"Thank goodness Phil came in, or I'd be there still. He pushed me out the kitchen door and up the hill by way of the terrace to my door. It was fun being out in the snow."

"What did Phil want?" Illi asked.

"He didn't say. I told him you were through with the books."

"Maybe it was your pretty brown eyes brought him," Mark teased. "Or maybe he's just got the habit, likes this house. I wouldn't blame him after that barn he lives in."

"That's what Mother said," Ardis replied. "She wanted him to stay for dinner but he said he couldn't. He seemed awfully uneasy. I feel sort of sorry for him."

"So do I," said Illi. "He's lonely. I think that's why he turns to books."

"Oh, he'll be all right when he gets away from his horsy family," Mark said. "He goes to Princeton next year. He ought to find a lot of bookish people there."

After dinner Mrs. Enwright said she thought she'd better start wrapping gifts, and Illi and Ardis offered to help. Illi had never seen such gorgeous papers and ribbons. She was in her element, matching and contrasting colors.

"How different this is from last Christmas," she said suddenly. "Last year each of us at the Camp got a pair of woolen stockings, an orange and a chocolate bar. And for dinner we had chicken pot pie with more pot pie than chicken."

"And this year you will have turkey and fixings and nylons and lots of surprises, won't she, Mother?" Ardis said mysteriously.

Illi looked up in time to catch Mrs. Enwright give a warning shake of her head to Ardis. She smiled to herself. She thought she knew two of the surprises. She had a glimpse of the dressmaker's judy when it had been delivered, and she'd seen the length of soft yellow wool jersey in Ardis' drawer under her best slips. But she could put on a good act of surprise on Christmas morning.

"Maybe other people will be surprised, too," she said, thinking of the make-up mirror that Ardis could hook on her neck and see the back of her head as she dressed, and the soft driving gloves with the leather palms for *Mütterchen*, both gifts upstairs in her room. For Daddy Bill there was a new book on book collecting and for Mark a leather frame for his Mother's picture. She had had such a good time spending her money.

"What do you think of this combination?" she asked, holding up a striped paper and a bolt of cerise ribbon. "Is it too gay?"

"You can't be too gay for Christmas," Mrs. Enwright said, "but try that lime green first."

Illi's hand reached for the green ribbon and stopped, because she was aware that Mr. Enwright was standing in the door and looking at her in a most peculiar way. "Illi," he said, "did you know that my copy of *The Scarlet Letter*—the inscribed one—has disappeared?"

Illi jumped to her feet, scattering paper and ribbon. "No, it must be there. It was, just the other night. I put it back on its own shelf myself. Ardis saw me, did you not, Ardis?"

Ardis stared at her, trying to think. "I don't remember exactly," she said. "I remember seeing it—you were talking about how much it cost, enough to buy a good horse."

"But I put it back, I'm sure I did. Perhaps you have not been looking in the right place, Daddy Bill," she said. "Shall I take a look for it?"

"I wish you would," he said, a worried frown on his face. "I found a buyer for that book today and I can sell at quite a nice profit. I'd like to close the deal before Christmas."

Illi followed him from the room. Back of her was silence and she could feel Ardis and her mother staring at each other in a puzzled, half-frightened way. She went directly to the shelf where *The Scarlet Letter* should have been. It was not there, not even the space where it might have been.

"It must be here somewhere," she said, taking out the

books to look behind them. "I could swear I put it back right here—and who else would have touched it?"

She stood looking around the tidy room, at the desk and table and chairs where books were no longer strewn. "I'll find it," she said stubbornly, "because it must be here," and she started making the rounds of the shelves.

"You're quite sure you will, Illi?" Daddy Bill asked in a way as if he knew the answer to his question.

"Of course. Are you sure, Daddy Bill, that you didn't take it out and put it somewhere else?"

"Illi, I haven't seen that book since I turned the place over to you and Phil. I was afraid something like this would happen. Could it have been thrown out or burnt up with some trash?"

"Oh no! There was no trash and I saw it here myself. So did Ardis."

"Did Ardis actually see the book or did she just hear you talking about it?"

"She saw it. I showed her and Phil the inscription."

"What was all this about buying a good horse?"

Illi laughed nervously. "Phil and I were comparing books and horses and I—I said that a lot of your books were worth as much as a good horse, and I pulled *The Scarlet Letter* off the shelf to prove it. I think Ardis was surprised."

"Funny she can't remember seeing you put it back," Mr. Enwright said thoughtfully.

Then the implication of the whole thing struck her. Her knees shook and her heart thumped with such fear as she had not known for a long time. "You mean—you do not believe me?" she gasped.

"I didn't say that," Mr. Enwright said. "If I inferred

it, I apologize. But you must realize that this is a serious thing, Illi. A book does not just walk out by itself. Think. Somebody must have taken it, unless you put it in the wrong place."

"But I didn't—wait! Phil might remember. He was the one who handed it back to me. Maybe he saw what I did with it."

"We'll find out." Mr. Enwright reached for the phone. In a few moments he was talking to Phil. Illi sank down on the edge of a chair because her knees would no longer hold her. Phil must remember, he must, she thought, listening to the one-sided conversation at the phone.

"So you gave it back to Illi, that right? . . . Did you see her put it away in its right place? . . . You're sure of that? . . . Well, it will probably turn up. Thank you, Phil."

He hung up and turned to Illi. "He said he handed it back to you and he felt very sure you put it back here on the shelf." He sat at his desk, turning his glasses over and over as he must have been turning over the problem in his mind. "It doesn't seem possible, but it begins to look as if someone had come in here later and helped himself. Someone who knew the value of that particular book, and where to sell it. He, or she, would have to know the names of the dealers."

"But—how—where—" Illi stammered.

"They are all there, in my little red book," he said simply and stared at her as if seeking the answer in her eyes.

"Will you—call the police?" Illi asked in a shaky voice.

144

"Not right away. We'll give it time to turn up, as it very well might. I've lost books before and found them months later. This may have been misplaced in spite of what you and Phil say."

Illi could only just sit and stare at him. She was still sure he did not believe her, he was giving her a chance to put the book back if she had not already disposed of it, and the knowledge lay like a weight on her heart. Fighting down the panic that rose within her she threw up her head and pulled herself up, standing tall and proud.

"I hope for your sake it does turn up," she said, and gulping down her sobs ran from the room. She went straight up the stairs to her own room and locked the door. There was a world out there she did not like. Then she threw herself on the bed and cried, ending in deep, racking sobs. It was as she had said to Ardis—always something happened to keep her from feeling happy and secure. Just at the point when she had begun to feel a part of this house, call it home in her own mind, she was rejected again, an outsider whom they could suspect as a thief. Why not? Hadn't she been a homeless girl who sometimes had had to steal to live? "Once a thief, always a thief," she could hear them saying. But why would she want to steal when she had everything she needed?

Of course they thought she had stolen the book to get money to buy Pokey from the Major. Were they talking about that downstairs now? Were they remembering all the things she had said about her determination to possess Pokey, to find the money somehow? Was Ardis telling her father again the exact words they had said in the study that day with Phil? Of course it all pointed to her, but had they no more faith in her than that? They had called her daughter, but would they have suspected Ardis, or Mark, or even Mrs. Grimm? Of course not, because they belonged here, everyone would trust them. She did not really belong to the Enwrights nor to anyone else. She was a stranger. She had no one who cared, no family of her own who would defend her. Oh, if she only knew where Janni was, if he was alive! She could go to him, back to the Old World if she had to. No matter how bad things were there, it would be better than this, to have to keep on living in a house where people suspected you of something you would never have done.

How long she lay there in the dark she did not know. She heard Mrs. Enwright come up the stairs and tap on her door but she didn't answer. What was there to say? The damage had been done. They had not believed her, they suspected her of being a thief. That could not be talked away. Even if they sent for the police it could be no worse than knowing how they felt. The police would have to release her for lack of proof—in this country Illi knew there had to be proof of guilt—but it could never undo what had been done by that look in Mr. Enwright's eyes.

She lay there on her bed without undressing, thinking, thinking, pulling the covers over her as the house cooled off. One thing she knew, she could not stay here any more. A plan began to form in her mind. She would leave before they could stop her, before she had to face those accusing faces in the morning, but first she would go down to the study and take one more good look for the book. If she found it she could lay it on Mr. Enwright's desk as if to say, "See? You were wrong, it was here all the time. Now aren't you sorry?" That was the only way she could hit back, save her pride.

She took off her shoes and slipped through the upper hall to the stairs. She could hear the murmur of voices in Mr. and Mrs. Enwright's room as she passed. They were still talking about her. Well, let them talk. She was through. She was on her own again or she would be in a few hours. She must not let herself think of all they had done for her. She must be strong, tough.

Before she turned on the study light she shut the door of the study carefully. Then she went through the shelves of books, one by one, moving them to look behind them. But she knew it was useless. The book would not be there unless, of course, Mr. Enwright in his absentminded way had thrust it in the wrong place. But she kept on. Finally she was sure; there was no sign of the book. She got down off the step-stool and stood there looking at Mr. Enwright's desk. Should she leave a note? No, that would be undignified. And what would she say?

She stood there wiping her hands, dusting them off, as if she would have liked to dust off the whole nasty business. Back of her she heard the door open quietly and she stood rooted with fear. Maybe it was the thief, come back for more loot, or to replace the book perhaps. But it was Mark's voice she heard saying, "Oh, so it's you!"

She swung around to face him. His sleepy eyes were

blinking at the light, his hair was tousled, and he was wearing a top coat over his pajamas. In one hand he had a flashlight and in the other a gun.

"What do you want?" she cried.

"I saw the light and I thought I'd better investigate. What on earth are you doing here, Illi?"

"I came to look for the lost book. You heard about it, no doubt?"

"Yes, I heard. A lot of fuss over nothing it seems. Have you found it?"

"No. It isn't here. Someone has taken it. Did you?"

"I? What would I want with an old book like that? Illi, have you gone out of your senses?"

"No, but somebody has. The book is gone. I did not take it, but they think I did."

"You're crazy. No one said a word about your taking it—"

"Maybe they are not saying it, but they are thinking it." She shrugged and started to push past him but he blocked her way.

"Illi, you're too sensitive. Nobody is accusing you. Why would they? They might just as well accuse me or Mrs. Grimm. It is too soon to accuse anyone. The book will turn up."

"But it will be too late," Illi said. Her eyes were fastened on the big pocket of his overcoat. Would it be big enough to hide a book? Was it there now? Had he come back to return it, if he still had it? Or had he sold it that very day before she met him for lunch. Mark's allowance was not large, yet he seemed to have had plenty for Christmas presents. Then she caught herself up guiltily. Why, here she was, suspecting Mark just

148

as Mr. Enwright had suspected her. A slow flush rose to her cheeks.

"I'm sorry, Mark," she said impulsively.

"Sorry? For what?" He had not apparently caught her look nor read her mind.

"Sorry about the whole thing. I'd like to go to my room now, if you please. Good night."

He stood aside to let her pass and she went out and up the stairs to her room. There she worked quietly, packing only the very few things she would need. She would take with her from the Enwrights' bounty only what she had to. Her savings had been depleted by her Christmas shopping but there was still enough to get her to the city.

Then she sat down and waited, watching the clock, timing her going so that she could catch the early bus that went past the road on the highway about six. When it was five-thirty she put on her coat and galoshes and gloves and taking the small bag went out the door to the hillside. The snow had stopped and the night was clear and starry now. She drew a deep breath of the wintry air and went down the hill to the drive. And because she could not bear to say good-by, she did not look back at the silent house set so securely against its hill.

Chapter 14

SHE STOOD WAITING at the bus stop, shivering, for the early morning air was piercing cold. No cars passed. She was alone in a white, empty world. It seemed she had waited a long time, almost an hour, when she heard a church bell tolling for early service. She remembered then, it was Sunday and there would be no early bus to accommodate the workers in the mills as there was on week days. There was nothing to do but walk to town. She bent her head against the wind and started on the four miles that lay ahead. Once in a while a car passed but she kept her head down and plodded on. She felt almost as if she were back in Germany in the old days, for this is the way it had so often been. Only then she did not have warm boots and gloves and fur at her neck.

It took her a good hour to reach town. It was still deserted in Sunday quiet. There was nothing to do but sit in the railroad station and wait for the first train to the city. She hoped her departure would not be noticed at the Enwrights' before she got away. The train she waited for came through from the west and as it stopped soldiers from the western camps piled off, coming home on Christmas leave. One soldier just like the rest was almost upon her before she saw who it was: Tom Grimm! She darted behind a baggage truck just in time and waited until he got past. Then she had to run for the train but she made it with the conductor's help.

"Close shave," he said with a smile.

"Yes," she said. He didn't know how close, because she knew Tom would never have let her get away.

She had never seen the city on Sunday. So many places were closed it looked very different from the jammed and crowded place she had seen only yesterday. She had as yet no clear idea of what she was going to do except to get herself a place to stay and a job to support her. She had thought of going further away, to some strange place, New York even, but she was afraid it would take too much of her money. This would do for a while.

She went into a clean-looking restaurant to get something to eat. A kindly-looking older woman waited upon her and Illi was moved to ask her if she could suggest a place to stay, one that was not expensive.

"How long are you planning to stay?" the woman asked.

"For some time, I think."

"Well, then there's no use trying the YW. They're full up except for transients." She looked at Illi, taking in her clothes and neat appearance. "I've got a room, it was my son's. He's in the Navy right now. I wasn't going to rent it but you seem like a nice girl, and if you don't want anything fancy . . ."

Illi said she did not want anything fancy. "Just clean and comfortable. Is it far from here?"

The woman, a Mrs. Porter, said no, and that her daughter would be home. She'd give her a call and Illi could go out there right away.

The little room at Mrs. Porter's was clean and comfortable but that was all. It had one window looking off over the roofs and chimneys but Illi told herself she was lucky. Now all she had to do was wait until tomorrow to get a job. But this room was no place to wait in. It gave her too much time to think, and she did not want to do that.

She went out to the sunny streets, now full of late churchgoers. She had not been in a church for years. At home her parents had always gone to church, but that was so long ago and the Enwrights belonged to no church, though Mrs. Enwright was always saying they really should join the congregation that met in the little stone chapel down at the crossroads. Illi thought it a pity so few people seemed to belong to any church in this country where freedom of worship was one of the great privileges. Maybe that was the trouble with the whole world, she thought, with her, with all of them. Maybe the world had turned its back on God and God was showing it that it could not move the right way without Him.

So she followed the crowd on the sidewalk to the doors of the big church opposite the city square. The service was just beginning and the big organ was rolling as she slipped into a pew at the back and bent her head. Nobody noticed her, nobody thought it strange that a young girl, well dressed and pretty, should be wiping tears from her eyes. Nobody heard the whispered words, "Dear God, bring Janni back to me—he's all I have now." She followed the service and listened to the sermon which was on the Lord's Prayer and the forgiving of trespasses, thinking of what she had done in turning her back upon the people who had befriended her, even though they had distrusted her.

She went out into the winter sunshine, a great part of the day still before her, and she wandered aimlessly through the streets, looking in windows, hesitating before a movie because she did not want to spend the money. At the railroad station she hesitated again. The thought crossed her mind: "I can still go home. I can say I just came to the city to church. They do not have to know I ran away." But she kept on with her walking. The thing was done now, she must see it through. Going home would not fix what was wrong.

At the steps to the public library she went in. The reading room was open for people like herself who had no other place to go. She picked up an armful of magazines and took a chair at a long table where she sat down to finish out the day. Hours later she realized that it was dark outside and she was hungry.

She stopped at the same restaurant for some dinner but Mrs. Porter was not there. Then she went home and to bed. It was the first time she had been alone for years; and where once she had liked the idea of being completely on her own with no one to tell her what to do or where to go, now she felt suddenly forlorn, lost. "This will never do," she told herself. "You will be alone now and you must learn to take it."

She fell into a deep sleep but it was a troubled one. She went from one dream to another, and in the last she was with Ardis. Ardis was in her wheel chair and it was being pushed by two policemen toward the edge of a cliff. She tried to call out to warn Ardis, but nothing came from her throat. Then she ran after the chair, but she could not catch up with it. It kept getting closer and closer to the rim but before it went over she woke up. She was drenched with perspiration and was shaking terribly. It was a long time until she could get back to sleep again.

But she woke early and was at the door of one of the big stores before it opened. It wasn't hard to get a job with Christmas only a few days away and the shopping still heavy. Many of the saleswomen had given out in the frantic rush of shoppers and the management was glad to find a fresh young girl as a replacement. They put her in the book department because she said she knew books. Even here it was rush and confusion. "A book for a man who likes dogs," "a book please for an old lady in a wheel chair," "a book about deep-sea fishing," and so on. A few she knew, a lot she had to guess at or inquire about, but she kept on for the full day, giving cheerful attention and service until she thought her back would break. Her feet felt like two huge blisters. That night she slept without dreaming and the next, and the next. Then it was Christmas Eve and the store was to close early to give the workers a chance to get ready for their own Christmases.

Most of the extras were being paid off, as they would not be needed after the Christmas rush, but as the girl came around distributing the envelopes, there was none for Illi.

"Why am I left out?" Illi asked.

"Aren't you a regular?" the girl asked in reply. "Maybe you better see the section manager."

Illi saw the section manager who was a brusque but kindly woman. "Oh, I forgot to tell you. The buyer in the book department asked me to see that you got put on our permanent basis—that is, if you want to stay. She liked your work. Says you're intelligent."

Illi said she would be glad to stay and left the store feeling as if one of her problems was solved. But she was too tired to eat. Later, after she had changed and rested, she would go out and get herself a dinner. She would be eating alone on Christmas Eve.

The little house glowed with lights as she let herself in with the key Mrs. Porter had given her. There was laughter and music in the small parlor off the hall. Mrs. Porter stuck her head out the door:

"Oh, it's you, Miss Horvath. I thought perhaps you'd be going home, or somewhere, for Christmas. Won't you join us? We're trimming the tree early so Jacky, my grandson, can enjoy it."

Illi was about to refuse, to say she was tired, but Mrs. Porter looked as though she would be disappointed and

155

she had been very kind. "Thank you," she said. "I'd like to see the tree. I can't stay too long though."

The little room seemed full of people though there was only Mrs. Porter's family, the single daughter, Grace, and the married daughter with her husband and little Jacky. He was sitting in a big chair, his legs stuck out straight in front of him. His eyes were shining with excitement but the legs—they were both in braces. Illi could not take her eyes away from them.

"Polio," his mother whispered as she handed Illi a cup of coffee. "But he's doing nicely now. The doctor says it's because we keep him so happy and contented. No invalid stuff for Jacky. It makes a great difference, he says."

Illi nodded. "I know," she said. "I have—I had—a friend the same way."

She sipped the coffee and ate a few of the little Christmas cakes and then she excused herself and went to her room. Those braces! Ardis was to have had her braces by Christmas, the doctor said. And here it was Christmas and perhaps Ardis had not got them. Maybe her running away had given Ardis a setback. Ardis was brave but she needed to be cherished and kept from worrying. And that had been Illi's job. And now there would be no Illi. They would have to find somebody else to stay with her and wait on her when Mrs. Grimm and her mother were not around. But would they be able to find anyone who loved her the way she, Illi, did? No matter what Ardis thought, or how she felt about Illi, she needed her now, right away.

And maybe Ardis had not suspected her at all, but maybe by this time she and Mrs. Enwright had both come to think Mr. Enwright was right because she had run away like a guilty one. Maybe she should have stayed and proved her innocence. After all, they had a good reason for suspecting her. She had wanted money so badly and who else could have taken the book? There was no one, except Mark. And she remembered that she had been just as bad as the Enwrights because she had suspected Mark with no proof either.

Before she could change her mind and talk herself out of it she began to pack her little bag. Then she left some money for Mrs. Porter and went quietly down the stairs and out of the house to the railroad station. She would go back and face the music, ask them to believe her just because she was Illi who loved them and owed them so much, tell them she understood why they thought her guilty, say she was sorry for having run out upon them like this and that she wanted to stay if they would have her back. It would be a hard thing to do. She would have to swallow all her pride, but it was the only thing to do. If they were through with her and didn't want her she could come back to the city, but she knew now that she should give them a chance to make the decision.

There was a train at eight and it met the late bus out to the road into the Enwrights'. As Illi walked up the lane from which the first beautiful snow had all melted, she thought it must have been more than just a few days since she'd walked down this lane in misery that early Sunday morning. She was still miserable, her throat was tight and her heart hammered at what lay before her. She wondered what she would say. She had thought of many things but nothing seemed right.

At the side door of the house she stopped, her feet refusing to carry her over the threshold. For a moment black panic swept over her and she half turned to go back. They might not understand why she had come, they might think she got cold feet, that she had found out it wasn't so easy to make your way alone, even in America. And how would she be able to tell them that it wasn't that at all, that she had come back because of Ardis and because common decency demanded that she should at least say thank you before they parted.

From inside she could hear music, Christmas carols on the radio, and the lights streaming from the living-room windows told her they were probably all gathered there. She ached to be with them, part of that warm, loving circle from which she had cut herself off because of her foolish pride. But her feet would not obey her.

Then she had an idea. Maybe her own door was still open. She went around the house and up the hillside and tried the knob. It was open. She went inside. It was just as she had left it. She washed her face and combed her hair and put on another dress, the one she was saving for Christmas. Then she went slowly down the stairs. In the hall she stopped again. She could hear their voices, Mr. Enwright, Mrs. Enwright, Ardis, and Mark. The music had been stopped. Apparently Mr. Enwright had just finished talking on the phone.

"Did you get the police? Didn't they have a single clue to her whereabouts?" she heard Mrs. Enwright say.

"Not a thing. I'd told them she might go down to Maryland, where you said, Ardis. They've put it on the teletype and are covering the area down that way."

"It was Neal who thought she might have gone down there to see that horse. But the Major telephoned there and they said no, there had been no sign of her. Oh, Daddy, what do you suppose has happened to her?"

"Now stop worrying." This was Mark. "Illi can take

care of herself all right. The thing is why did she do it— if she wasn't guilty of stealing that book?"

"I still say she didn't take it and nobody can make me believe that she did," Mrs. Enwright said stoutly.

"Nobody is trying to make you believe it, Petey," Mr. Enwright said. "It occurred to me for a moment, naturally, but when I thought of all the fine things we knew about Illi I was sure it was impossible."

"Of course it was impossible," Ardis said. "Illi couldn't steal a—a pin. That darn old book! All it did was get us into trouble." She began to cry and Illi could hear Mrs. Enwright rush to comfort her.

She took a deep breath and two steps forward into the living room. "Merry Christmas, everybody," she said, trying to put good cheer into it, but the words were a hoarse imitation of her usual voice.

"Illi!"

"It's Illi."

"She's come home!"

"Oh, Illi child, we have been frantic about you, simply frantic. We finally called in the police to help find you. Oh, Illi, Illi!" And then she was in Mrs. Enwright's arms and she, too, was crying and Mrs. Enwright was comforting her.

"I—I feel just—terrible," she wailed, "to have brought this worry upon you. It was a very silly thing to do. I know that now, and I'm so sorry."

"But why, Illi, why did you do it?" Ardis asked between her own sobs.

"It was my pride. I thought you all thought I had taken that book, and it hurt me so I—I just packed up and left. But I started to think about it. I went to church Sunday and then I saw a little boy—" she stopped suddenly and looked at Ardis who had a light blanket thrown over her knees. "Ardis," she asked, "*did* you get your braces?"

"Yes." Ardis lifted the blanket and displayed her legs encased in the ugly things of steel and leather. But to

Ardis they were beautiful. She was as proud of them as if they were two glass slippers or the seven-league boots. "I took four steps today. Tomorrow it will be five. In two weeks the doctor says I should be able to walk across the room. I can't wear them all day yet, but I will soon."

"Oh, you will, you will!" Illi cried, almost hysterical with joy. "I'll help you, Ardis. You'll see. We'll show them what we can do together."

It was late when the circle around the fire broke up and Illi climbed the stairs to her own room. She was smiling to herself at all the whispering and signs of conspiracy that had been going on down there. The Enwrights seemed to get as much fun out of getting ready for Christmas as for the actual festivities themselves. Once Mr. Enwright had asked, "Have you told her?" and Mrs. Enwright quickly shushed him with a murmured, "Not yet, not until Christmas."

"Well, it's pretty nearly that now," he'd said with a glance at the clock.

"I know. That's what I mean," his wife had said and left the room. They could hear her steps moving back and forth overhead.

"What's it all about?" Illi had whispered to Ardis.

"Wait and see. I think you are going to get the best surprise of all, Illi."

But she did not know how truly Ardis had spoken until she reached her room. Moonlight in a silver path across her floor fought with the low bed lamp lighting her pillow. It was so beautiful she wanted to undress in the dark so she could look out on the snowy hillside with its hemlocks bending heavy with snow. She went

161

to turn out the small bedside lamp—and then she saw it. It was an envelope of thin blue paper with a spidery foreign writing upon it. It bore an Austrian stamp and Janni's name in one corner. She tore it open with shaking fingers and hurriedly scanned the Hungarian words that now seemed almost strange to her:

Dear little sister,

I have at last found out your whereabouts. It has taken me a long time, but the various agencies have been very kind and patient with me. It was actually through some of your army officers that I got news of you. I have been told that you have found a good home with kind American people and it makes me very happy. I too would like to come to America some day. Right now I am teaching skiing at a little mountain village in the Bavarian Alps. It looks like home and I would like it if I did not yearn to see you and also to make more of my life. I meet many of your American GI's here and I am speaking English now fluently. They make good friends. I am hoping by next winter that I can get to America, if not on the quota at least on a temporary visa as a ski instructor. Then we can see each other and embrace after all these long years, and I will tell you the story of my wanderings, which is too long to put down here.

I am sending you a photograph that one of the soldiers took of me. Would you know your old Janni? War and privation make one look much older, but I am one of the lucky ones who survived.

Please write to me at once and tell me all about yourself. Are you married? Have you a sweetheart? And send me a picture of yourself. I still think of you as the little wildcat rider on the back of Vidám. Remember him?

Your loving brother,
Janni

She held the snapshot under the light and turned it in her fingers taking in every detail of the tall, dark stranger in the leather jerkin, leather ski pants, the heavy boots and the tassels below the knee. Only the eyes looked like Janni. They were smiling right at her the way they used to do and she smiled back at them.

"Oh, Janni, Janni," she murmured, half laughing, half crying. "You look as old as Methuselah, but with those eyes you will never grow up."

She laid the letter down and went to her door to spread the news to the family. But the house was silent. It would have to wait. She knew now that *Mütterchen* had planned it this way so she could be alone with her new-found joy. She could cry all she liked and nobody would make fun of her. She turned out the light and went to stand at her window looking out at the snowy hillside with the tears running down her cheeks like the little brook through its icy banks.

It was so quiet out there. She felt she could almost hear the stars moving in the clear midnight sky. It must have looked like this on that hillside in Bethlehem when the shepherds heard the angels singing. And now her heart was singing, too, a hymn of thankfulness for Janni, for her own, darling family, for the sudden impulse that had made her lower the flag of her pride and sent her back home for Christmas. She didn't deserve this happiness, but she would try to earn it.

163

As she lay warm and snug and safe under her soft yellow blankets she thought, "I feel right inside now. I know I am truly wanted. I've been stupid not to see it before. I guess I'm like Ardis. I want people to love me, not just be sorry for me. Oh, God, please keep them wanting me! I could never go on again alone."

Chapter 15

EVERYONE WAS UP early on Christmas morning. "It's almost as bad as when Ardis was a little girl," Mrs. Enwright said, coming into Illi's room to wish her a Merry Christmas and follow it with a hearty kiss. "She's been ringing her bell trying to get us up."

"I know. I heard it. I was just going down to see if she wanted something," Illi said.

"She just wants us to hurry. She can't wait. This is a big day for Ardis. In fact for all of us. You see we're quite a family today, five of us counting Mark. If you'll go down and start the coffee, Illi, I'll go over to the barn and get that sleepyhead of a Mark up. I think we should install a fire siren over there."

Illi laughed. "Even that might not do it," she said. "Mark could sleep through anything."

"Yes, I guess he has a clear conscience." Mrs. Enwright came over to where Illi was combing her hair and put her hands on her shoulders. "There's something I want to tell you, Illi, while we're still alone. I want you to know how I appreciated your coming back in time for this day. Everything would have been spoiled for Ardis if you hadn't."

"I know," Illi said huskily. "That's why I did it, not just—just for myself. I've been afraid you would think I just got cold feet and . . ."

"No, I didn't think that for one moment. I know that stubborn little pride of yours, and I know how hard it was for you to—well, as we say over here, eat crow."

"Eat crow? What does that mean?"

"It means to admit you were wrong. That takes courage. I think you have it, Illi."

"I'm glad I came back now, but I was afraid at first. I could have stayed you know. I had a job. They want me to come back tomorrow as a permanent saleswoman in the book department."

"That sounds like a real achievement, Illi. Do you want to go back?"

"No, not if you really want me to stay after all that has happened. I can phone the store tomorrow."

"But of course we do. Now I must get downstairs . . ."

"Wait just a minute, *Mütterchen*," Illi stopped her at the door. "I didn't tell you about my letter."

"Was it good news? I've been afraid to ask."

"It is wonderful. It was from Janni. He's safe in

166

Austria and well, and wants to come to America next year."

"Fine. I hoped that was it. The letter came the day after you left and I felt so badly it had not come earlier. Perhaps if it had you would not have run away."

Illi's comb stopped its arc through her bright hair. "Please don't make excuses for me, *Mütterchen*. Maybe it was a good thing I did what I did—it sort of cleaned out things in my mind—the wrong things."

Mrs. Enwright nodded understandingly. "Yes, you may be right. But I am glad you have heard from your brother. We were so afraid they would not be able to trace him."

"We? You mean you were trying to find him for me?" Illi asked in astonishment.

"Yes, in a way. But it was really through Mark's father. Mark wrote to him about you and Janni and asked him to see what he could do. Mark felt if Janni wasn't dead or in a Russian prison camp he would probably be in Austria or Germany."

"Mark? He took all that trouble? Why, I never thought Mark cared enough about me or my affairs to do that."

"Mark has a lot of good points. And he's learning to think about other people. Maybe that's because he has had such a good example living right beside him." She smiled at Illi. "I mean a certain person not six feet away."

Illi flushed. "I wasn't thinking about anybody but myself the other night," she said guiltily. "I don't deserve to be treated the way you have treated me, so kind —so understanding . . ." her voice broke.

"We have only wanted you to be happy, Illi dear," Mrs. Enwright said. "And now that you know about your brother, I am sure you will be. It must have seemed like a miracle."

"Oh, it was. I prayed you know," she said solemnly and with a sort of wonder. "I prayed that Sunday in the city in the cathedral. I prayed that Janni would prove to be alive and that we would see each other again. And now my prayer has been answered—at least part of it, the part that matters. Oh, *Mütterchen*, you have no idea how happy I am inside." She threw herself into the waiting arms of Mrs. Enwright.

"I'm happy, too," Mrs. Enwright said, wiping away a few tears. "I've always been afraid that you might want to go back to Europe to try to find Janni."

Illi shook her head. "No, I won't do that, not now. I love Janni, he's all that is left of the old life, but I don't need him the way I thought I did. I can be patient and wait for the rest of the miracle now."

"Good girl! Now we really must get downstairs—and oh, Illi, don't mention that book to Daddy Bill, please. He feels so bad about it. He says he never wants to hear about it again. You know, maybe I shouldn't tell you this but I think you should know it. He was going to ask the Major to put a price on Pokey and if he could meet it, he was going to sell that book and buy the horse for you as a Christmas surprise."

"What?" Illi swung around to stare at her open-mouthed.

"Yes. He wanted to do something especially nice for you. He was so proud of the job you had done for him.

But we don't have the kind of money to buy blooded horses . . ."

"But to sell one of his prized books! That would have been terrible. He loves his books."

"Oh, I don't think there are many he feels that strongly about. Many of them are just investments. He buys and sells all the time. He says they are like bonds in the bank. Sometimes he finds them in old bookshops and picks them up for a song and then sells them for a good price to dealers or collectors. It's quite a business as well as a hobby. Just like horse-trading, I guess."

"Well, I'm glad he didn't sell that book to buy Pokey for me. I would have felt so uncomfortable if he had. I love Pokey but not that much."

Mrs. Enwright smiled. "Well, he's a nice little horse, so Neal says. Maybe some time you'll find one you can afford."

"Maybe, but he won't be like Pokey. But do you know," her hand with the comb stopped in midair, "I believe I can get along without Pokey now. He is not so important to me. I am not so lonely."

"Well! Those are sweet words, the nicest Christmas present I could wish for." Mrs. Enwright blew her a kiss in the glass. "Now let's go downstairs and fill those hungry people who are waiting for us. Then we can have the presents."

It was a beautiful Christmas. The presents in their bright wrappings under the glistening tree were given out by Daddy Bill, who proved a very amusing Santa Claus without benefit of beard or red flannel. Illi was duly "surprised" when the dressmaker's judy was unveiled and the package of yellow wool jersey opened.

But when Daddy Bill handed her an envelope and told her to put it in the "Pokey fund" she was reduced to tears because it was a check for twenty-five dollars.

"I wish it could have been more," he said. "But plant it carefully and maybe it will grow."

"She's crying," said Mark. "Catch me crying if someone handed me a check like that."

"It's just a way of being happy," Illi said, wiping away her tears. "You know they say that we Hungarians amuse ourselves with our tears. We like to cry."

"We Hungarians! There you go again," Mark said disgustedly. "When are you going to call yourself a good American, Illi?"

"Some day, some day very soon, because now I am beginning to feel like an American in my heart."

It was still early when she finished the breakfast dishes. Mrs. Grimm had been given the day off to spend with her own family, but she had made everything ready for the Christmas dinner, turkey ready for the oven, pies baked.

Illi said, coming into the living room where Daddy Bill and Mark were down on the floor watching the crazy wind-up auto Mark had got in his stocking, "I think I should like to go to church. Would you drive me into Waverly in the jalopy, Mark?"

Mark jumped to his feet. "You bet," he said. "Get your coat."

"I wonder if Geegee goes to church," Ardis said idly. "It would be so nice if she did."

"That I wouldn't know," Mark said, but he went off whistling to get the jalopy warmed up.

The Christmas service was short but Illi felt she had

come closer to God by coming to worship in His house. She had wanted to say thank you in a special way for Janni, for all the people who had been so good to her. At the church door Mark detained her and she knew that she had not been wrong when she thought she saw Geegee's head bobbing up in front.

"Hi! Merry Christmas!" Geegee said and introduced her family. Then she said to Illi, "What happened to you this week? Someone said you'd run away, that the police were looking for you."

"We heard it on the radio," Mrs. Fairchild explained.

"Nothing to it," Mark explained quickly with a warning look for Illi. "All a mistake. Illi had business in the city and it took her longer than she thought it would. Uncle Bill got worried and called the police, but she got home all right."

"I wondered," Geegee said. "Who could possibly want to run away from a place like the Enwrights'."

"Well, I'm going to run away tonight to a place called the Fairchilds', if I may?" Mark said with a look at Geegee's mother. "Did you hang that mistletoe where I told you to?"

Geegee giggled and with another flurry of Merry Christmases from her family they passed on.

"Thank you, Mark," Illi said as she climbed into the jalopy. "You saved my life. I would not have known what to say."

"Oh, I know how to manage Geegee. She'll believe anything I tell her."

"Then see that you tell her the right things," Illi said.

"Okay, teacher, I will," Mark said and turned the car toward home.

171

Ardis was popping with excitement when they came into the living room. "Guess what? Neal and his mother and the Major are coming over for dinner. Mother insisted on it. And then we are to go over there for New Year's Eve. Won't that be fun?"

"Yes," Illi said. "I'll run up and change so I can help *Mütterchen.*" But on her way to the door she asked, "Does Neal know about me—that I ran away?"

"Of course. We called him right away because we thought he might know something about it. But of course he didn't. He was just as worried as we were and just as glad you're home, too. I called him first thing this morning. Illi, I think Neal likes you very, very much."

Illi flushed. "Now, Ardis," she said, "remember what I told you about Neal."

"I remember, but I'm not so sure it's true. I think Neal may *want* not to have a special girl right now, but maybe he can't help liking one better than the rest."

"You're dreaming again."

"Yes, but I'm dreaming for you this time, Illi. Because I know you won't dream for yourself. You're too busy thinking about other people."

Illi laughed. "That is the first time I ever heard of a—how do you say it?—stand-in for dreaming? But thank you, Ardis. I like Neal, too, but I think it is too soon for dreaming."

However what Ardis had said was very much on her mind as she helped Mrs. Enwright in the kitchen and set the big pine table in the living room with places for eight. She was just about to mash the potatoes when she heard the Major's car drive up, but she did not go out

172

to greet the guests. It was going to be hard to face Neal. She wondered what he would say to her about her running away.

Then someone came up behind her and put his hands over her eyes. "Guess who?" said a familiar voice.

"Neal! Don't you know better than to interrupt the cook?"

"Interrupt? Why you haven't stopped whacking those potatoes a second. Here give me that dinkus. I'm the best potato masher in the county."

She gave him the masher without meeting his eyes and went to stir the gravy bubbling on the stove.

For a minute the only sound in the kitchen was the mash-mash of Neal's husky efforts. Then he said, "Illi, why did you do it? Run away, I mean."

"I think I must have had a brainstorm," she said. "I was feeling very sorry for myself. I thought nobody loved me or trusted me and the way I behaved I wouldn't blame them now if they didn't."

"But you've changed your mind? You know now that they do love you and trust you?"

"Yes," she said simply. "I don't see why they do, I haven't done much to earn it, but I know it's true." She took a small pan of warm milk from the stove and poured it into the mashed potatoes. Then she added a lump of butter and pepper and salt. "Now, beat them some more with a fork, like this."

She stood for a moment watching Neal attack the potatoes. Then she said, "Neal, did you know I have found out about Janni. He's alive. I got a letter from him."

"No. Honest? Where is he?"

"He's in Austria, in the American zone. He's teaching all the GI's how to ski."

"So now I suppose you'll be moving heaven and earth to see him. You aren't thinking of trying to get back there yourself?" He whipped at the potatoes vigorously as if they were something that needed chastising.

"No, why should I do that, even if I could? It will be better if he comes to me—and he will. It may take a miracle to bring it about, but I'm getting used to miracles." She gave a little laugh and came over to drop another piece of butter into the potatoes. "An extra dab for Christmas," she said.

Neal stuck his finger in the mash and gave it to her to taste. "All right?" She nodded. He went back to the potatoes, not looking at her as he said, "You're a queer girl, but a nice one, Illi. You've changed a lot lately. Gosh, were you a stick when I first met you."

"And what am I now?" she asked, waiting with the gravy spoon dripping while her blue eyes dared him to say what she wanted to hear.

"You're a darn good sport to begin with and—stick around, please, Illi! Don't go running off again or I'll have heart failure and fail to pass my physical for the Point."

"I'll stick around," Illi said, bending over a steaming pot of broccoli to hide the smile on her lips. "I expect to be sticking around here for some time."

"For four years?"

"Maybe."

There was silence. The beating had stopped. She looked up to meet Neal's eyes upon her. And the look in them made her heart beat very fast.

174

"That's my girl," he said. "I think we understand each other fine, just fine." Then his hand went to his pocket. "Omygosh! I almost forgot this. Thought for a while that maybe I'd have to return it and get my money back." He tossed a small box to her. She laid down her spoon and opened it with shaking fingers. It was a small silver photograph frame and it held an enlarged snapshot of Pokey.

"From the boy friend himself," said Neal.

"From the boy friend, bless him," Illi said and planted a kiss on Pokey's nose.

"Hey, if you're handing out kisses how about me?" Neal dropped his fork and, coming over, kissed her soundly. "I always kiss my girls on Christmas," he said, "no matter how I treat them the rest of the year."

"I think you treat them very well, on the whole," Illi said. "If you'll tell me your kissing days, I shall mark them on my calendar."

"Cute!" Neal stood off to admire her. "You're a cute kid, getting cuter every day." He chucked her under the chin and picked up the fork again until the potatoes were a great foamy mass of white fluff.

Illi came to poke her nose into the pot and Neal put his arm around her. "Do they suit you, Madam Chef?"

"Yes," she said, making a face at him. "They suit fine."

"Hey, break it up!" It was Mark in the doorway and he was grinning appreciatively. "We're hungry out here."

Illi got the dinner assembled with the help of the two boys but she felt as if she were walking on pink clouds instead of red linoleum. And when her plate was filled by Daddy Bill she felt as if she were eating ambrosia rather than good brown turkey and fixings. Across the table Ardis gave her a big wink, and she knew that Ardis guessed what had gone on in the kitchen, that perhaps she had even sent Neal out to help.

"Why, I'm dreaming," she thought suddenly. "Now, Ardis won't have to do it for me." She drew a deep sigh. "And it's going to be a good, long dream, too, maybe as long as four years."

Chapter 16

FOUR THINGS HAPPENED in the week between Christmas and New Year's that were to make life for Illi different in several ways. The first came when Ardis and she were alone the day after Christmas for the first time. Ardis had seemed uneasy and Illi had wondered if she were still hurt at Illi's running off and leaving her. But she would not question her. If Ardis had something to say to her she must do it unassisted. At last it came out.

"Illi, I can't keep this thing to myself any longer," she said, pulling something from the pocket of the sports dress she was wearing. "Look!"

Illi looked. It was a ring on a thin gold chain, a simple

little ring of two twisted strands of gold rope. "Where did it come from?" she asked as she examined it, but she could guess the answer.

"From Tom. He had to go back Christmas morning, as you know, but he gave this to me Christmas Eve, just before you came back."

"Does it mean what I think it means?"

"Not exactly. He would like it to, but Daddy and Mother said no. He spoke to them first to ask them if they'd mind. He's very honorable, you know."

"Of course." Illi smiled at the soberness of the sweet face.

"They said they wouldn't think of allowing me to tie myself down, under the circumstances, nor of letting Tom do it either. Tom's old enough to know what he's doing, three years older than I am, but he's still young. And there is so much that can happen . . ." her voice faltered. "It looks as if he might be sent out of the country almost any time."

"Would you like to be tied down to waiting for Tom, Ardis?"

She nodded mutely. Then she said, "I'm used to being tied down. It wouldn't make it any worse and it might make it a lot better. But we agreed to do what Dad and Moms asked. So that's the way it is. I can't wear the ring but I can keep it as a, well, a sort of reminder that I've *got* to get better *fast*. I've got to be walking without these when he comes home for good. And you've got to help me, Illi."

"I'll help, you know that," Illi said. She wished she could tell Tom Grimm what a fine thing he had done for Ardis, because she knew he had brought things to a head purposely. It wasn't like Tom to rush things, but now he had given this girl he'd known and loved and admired for so long something to live for, to make the struggle for recovery even more important. And even if nothing came of it, if Ardis, able to lead the normal life of a girl of nineteen or twenty, should meet someone else she loved more, or if Tom—if Tom should not come back, it would still have been a good thing. But of course she did not say this to Ardis.

What she did say was, "I'm so glad, Ardis, so glad you have such a fine person to dream about now."

"And what about you, Illi? Are you dreaming, too?"

Illi nodded reluctantly. "A little. But I won't see much of Neal either. He takes the competitive examinations for his West Point appointment in March, you know, so he'll have to study like mad, especially his math. He's shaky on geometry."

"Oh dear! I hope he passes."

"He has to more than pass. He has to come out in the first forty, because they only provide forty cadetships to the sons of veterans of World War II."

"Do you think he will make it?"

"I don't know. It depends on how many others take it and how smart they are, I guess."

"I thought the Major would be able to do something for him," Ardis said. "I didn't think it would be so hard."

"The Major believes in the hard way," Illi laughed. "And I think he is right. Neal is apt to be too easy going. Now we shall see."

But she was as nervous as if she herself would be sitting in that big examination room in Washington a few months later. "We won't know until after Easter," Neal had said, "and maybe not then if they don't get the papers corrected. I am just glad my old math teacher from High isn't going to do the correcting. He'd find it hard to forget what a holy terror I was."

And so she had to wait through the long holiday week with nothing but a hasty call from Neal one evening. He seemed less worried. "I got caught up on a lot of required reading this week, Illi," he said, "and I think I've really got my teeth into the math too."

She had almost forgotten her own plans for next year until the evening Mrs. Enwright said, "I've been looking into art schools and courses for you, Illi. Of course if you want to go away to college we want you to go, but you should be entered as soon as possible. So I think it is time for you to make up your mind now."

"Oh, I've made it up—about college, I mean. I'd much rather not go, *Mütterchen*. I want to stay home with Ardis."

"But you will want to do something. There's a fine school in the city, the Poore Institute, that specializes in commercial art courses. You could go in with us every day—"

"But what about Ardis?"

"By that time I shall be able to wait on myself," Ardis said proudly. "I took two more steps today and I kept my braces on for the whole morning."

"That's what I meant," Mrs. Enwright said. "In another year we hope Ardis will be so much better that you can begin to think of yourself, Illi."

"She'll never do that," Ardis said with an impish grin. "If it isn't me it will be somebody else."

"There's a Poore catalogue in the study on my desk," Mr. Enwright put in. "Why don't you get it and go over it right now?"

"Is there anything in it about scholarships?" Illi asked.

"Yes, I believe there is. But don't worry about the scholarship. If you get one, all right, but if you don't, we are prepared to send you—that is if you want to go."

So Illi went to the study. She had not been in it since the night when she had run away. When she passed the door she would turn her eyes away because she did not want to be reminded of what had happened there. Now she hesitated for a moment in the doorway, but calling herself silly she went in and straight to the desk where the catalogue was lying. She picked it up and started to leave the room. But in spite of herself her eyes strayed to the shelf where the lost book had been. Then she gasped with surprise. It was there—or else she was seeing things. It had been found. Why hadn't they told her?

Slowly she took it from the shelf and looked inside to make sure that it was the same book. It was. Daddy Bill had said there was only one with an inscription like that. Where had it come from? Where had it been? If someone had put it back, who? There had been a lot of people in and out of the house during the holidays, Tom and Mrs. Grimm of course, the Major and Mrs. Austin, Neal, the Prentices, both Phil and Peachy, Geegee and her mother, all making holiday calls, but all of them seemed as impossible of taking it, or even of borrowing it, as she had been. She turned the pages of the book, wondering if she should call it to Daddy Bill's attention or do as *Mütterchen* had said, not mention it at all, let him find it himself, if he had not already done so.

Then she saw the small piece of paper between the pages. She picked it up and examined it. It was a piece of notepaper with *Norwood Farms* engraved at the top and on it were scribbled notes on American literature in a hand she had become familiar with—Phil's. So it was Phil who had taken it! The temptation had been too much for him.

She was shocked, yet at the same time she felt sorry for him. She could imagine how he must have felt when he learned or guessed that she had been suspected of taking it. He couldn't have come right out that night on the phone and told on himself. That was asking too much of a boy without too much backbone to begin with. Well, at least Daddy Bill had his prized book back and that was something. But how would she tell him?

Then she knew she was not going to tell him at all. She would just have to let him think what he would. If he still believed she had taken it and replaced it, that would be too bad, but she was so sure now that no matter how things pointed to her he would never suspect her again, she was willing to risk it. In time he might even arrive at the truth, but she wasn't going to help him.

She put the book back on the shelf in its regular place, then on second thought she pulled it out beyond the others just a bit so it would be noticeable. She took the incriminating piece of paper and tore it into little bits and went back to the living room. There she went straight to the fireplace and threw the small pieces of Phil's tattletale paper on the fire.

"Burning love letters?" Mark asked.

"No," she said, "just some scrap notes that were not important. I keep my love letters, all tied up with blue ribbons, to console me when I am an old, despairing spinster."

"Spinster! Fancy that!" he laughed. "You have the mark of a girl who is going to marry young, I can always tell," he gibed. "I bet you're working on your trousseau already."

Mrs. Enwright looked up from her book and Mr. Enwright dropped his paper.

"Don't talk nonsense," Illi told Mark, but her face showed the embarrassed blush and Daddy Bill and *Mütterchen* raised their brows and exchanged glances.

She wondered how much she showed of her inner dreaming when they gathered at the Major's for the

New Year's Eve celebration. This time they were entertained in the big double parlors at the front of the house. Mrs. Austin, looking very much the gracious hostess in a dress of soft blue silk, bustled around caring for everyone's comfort. The Major beamed upon everybody. There were other guests, most of whom Illi did not know except the Prentices. Peachy was staying close to Neal. It was Phil who rushed over to greet her with a great show of cordiality.

"Gosh," he said, "I'm glad to see you. I didn't know you had run off until Geegee told me."

Illi flushed. "That Geegee! I thought Mark had fixed that rumor. He told her it was all a mistake."

Phil nodded. "That's what she said, but—*did* you run away, Illi?"

"Yes," she said simply. "And I think you know why, Phil."

He looked away from her uneasily. "Why would I?" he said.

"I found the lost book yesterday, Phil, and there was a piece of paper in it."

"Paper? What kind of paper?" he asked, alarm in his eyes.

"A scrap of Norwood notepaper with your writing on it."

"Oh. What—what did you do about it?"

"I burned it. And I put the book back in its place. That's all I did about it and all I intend to do."

He turned to face her and grasped both her hands in a hearty gesture. "Gee, thanks, Illi, thanks a lot! I've been worried sick about that book. I don't know why I took it, but my fingers just itched to possess it, to see it on my

own bookshelves. It was so easy, nobody was around—
they were all in the kitchen. And then Mr. Enwright
phoned me—and I knew it had been missed. I'd have put
it back right away but I couldn't. Then I heard you had
gone off and—well, you'll never know how I felt until I
got it back. Will you forgive me, Illi?"

"I have nothing to forgive," Illi said, "but I have something to say. Please, Phil, don't let anything get you to
the point of stealing or pulling shabby tricks again.
Nothing is worth it, not even books—or a good horse.
You can buy those but you can't buy back a good char-
acter."

"I guess you're right, Illi. I've learned my lesson. I
think a lot of you, you know, and I wouldn't want you
blamed for something I did. How about making the
rounds of that buffet table? Looks good to me."

They came back from the dining room to find the
Major holding forth to his guests from his stand against
the fine Adam mantel in the living room.

"It's a long time since I filled this room with such
good friends," he said, waving his cup of punch jovially.
"I must do it often. A house goes to pieces when it isn't
used the right way. Isn't that right, May?" He looked at
Mrs. Austin who answered him with a shy smile.

Illi thought suddenly, "Why, she's pretty and young,"
and she wondered if perhaps the Major was thinking the
same thing. Maybe by this time next year Mrs. Austin
would be the real lady of the house. Maybe that was
why the Major had taken such an interest in Neal.

"I invited you folks here for a neighborly New Year's
get-together," he was saying. "But it so happens I have
another reason for celebrating. I want to present to you

185

all the future Mrs. Wallace, my good friend and guardian angel, May Austin."

Everyone exclaimed at once and went to shake the Major's hand and say nice things to Mrs. Austin, who, smiling and blushing, kept her hand on the Major's arm as if afraid he might desert her. Peachy lingered to tuck her arm possessively in Neal's, but Illi, watching from across the room, caught Neal's broad wink and returned it in kind. Then she followed Mrs. Enwright to the kitchen to give Neal's mother a last-minute help with the refreshments.

It was some time later when Illi felt a hand on her elbow and heard the Major say, "Young lady, I'd like a word with you in private, if you please."

Chapter 17

ILLI SAT FACING the Major in his office, a very practical room with a roll-top desk, where he managed the affairs of his farm. Her heart was beating furiously because she could not imagine why he had called her there. Did it have anything to do with her running away? Or was the Major going to warn her not to interfere with Neal's career? As if she would!

But there was nothing frightening about his voice as he said, "I thought we could talk better here. I wanted to say something about that horse."

"Pokey? Or should I say Hocus-pocus?"

"Yes, Pokey, the colt who seems to have taken such a

fancy to you. First of all I want to ask you this—have you ever done any jumping?"

"Yes, some. I had begun to jump back at Kisber. Old Geza, the groom who taught me to ride, was teaching me that too. He said he wanted to make an all-round horsewoman of me."

"That was a long time ago. Do you think you could jump now?"

"I think so. I believe it would not be long until I could."

"Have you had any experience in schooling a horse?"

"Only with Vidám, my own colt, while we were both learning to jump. But I've watched it done often."

The Major nodded. "Well, it's evident you know horses and love them and that counts for a lot. Here is what I have in mind. That little colt was a gift to me, as I think I told you. I can't afford to keep a horse around here that doesn't earn his keep and stable room in some way. Now I want to see what this Pokey will do. I think perhaps he will make a good hunter. Neal says he shows signs of it now. I can't bother with him myself and Neal won't have the time to spend on him, so I've been wondering how you would like to take him on, school him for me."

"I'd love it," Illi said, her eyes shining.

"Well, that's fine. I'll speak to Mrs. Enwright about it. I think she's sensible. It may mean a spill or two for you and it's going to take time, too. We'll have to start right off, snatching the fair days when there is no snow so we can be in shape for the Hospital Horse Show in May."

"Oh, you mean you are going to enter him in a show?"

"Yes. I don't often bother, but they keep after me to do it. I go in for race horses, but occasionally I get a good riding horse or a jumper or a hunter good enough to show. It's a worthy cause and good business, I guess. I think this Pokey will probably make the Green Hunter Class. We'll know better when you get working with him."

Illi hurried to tell Neal what the Major had said.

"I know, he spoke to me about it," Neal said. "Do you really want to do it?"

"Do I want to? What a silly question! But, Neal, you'll have to help me just a little at first. I'm a bit scared. It seems like such a big job, and I haven't done much jumping . . ."

"Oh, you'll manage all right. I'll get Tim and Jake, two of our best grooms, to keep an eye on you if I can't be around. I hoped you'd be pleased about this, Illi. The next best thing to owning Pokey is schooling him and showing him in the ring, isn't it?"

"Yes. Especially as it means the Major won't be selling him off, not right away at any rate."

"Incidentally, how would you like to take a day off and have fun with me this Saturday before I go back to the grind? I think the Major will let me have the car. We'll make a day of it."

"I'd love to if Ardis—"

"Now wait. I've been talking over this business about Ardis with her mother. She agrees with me that you can do too much for Ardis right now. She says you have done your job, given Ardis new hope and interest in

189

life. But Ardis has to learn to help herself. And she can. The more effort she puts out the better. So I don't want to hear any more excuses like that."

"All right," Illi said meekly. "I'll go with you Saturday. What are we going to do?"

"Wait and see," he said with a grin, "and pray it won't snow."

It did not snow on Saturday. In fact it was one of those days when it seems as if winter had changed its mind. It seemed queer to be riding with Neal in a car. They had not had many dates that did not include a horse. She watched his brown hands on the wheel and thought how capably Neal did everything, so surely and yet so easily. He would make a fine officer, she was sure of that.

"Are you terribly excited about those exams in March?" she asked him suddenly.

"Naturally. But after all, all I can do is to use the next two months to good advantage and do my best. Worrying isn't going to help."

"I don't believe you ever worry, do you, Neal?"

He gave her a swift glance. "You wouldn't have said that if you could have seen me those few days before Christmas," he said. "I ran around like a chicken with its head off trying to figure why you did it and where you went."

"Didn't they tell you anything about that book?"

"What book?"

"Never mind. I guess they didn't. And it doesn't matter now. Something happened and my pride got the best of me. I think I've lost a lot of that pride now, Neal."

"Don't lose it all. I like to see that little head of yours

190

go up with a jerk. I like a girl with some spirit and independence. How about stopping for lunch?"

They had lunch at an old inn in a raftered room with a big fire burning on the huge hearth. They were the only guests and it made the place seem cozy and intimate. Illi savored the old-time atmosphere, peopling the place with customers far different from Neal and herself. "Where are we, anyway?" she asked curiously when they were half through their hot turkey sandwiches.

"We're at the Rising Sun Inn, one of the oldest in Maryland."

"Maryland?" She looked at Neal and caught the spark of amusement in his eyes. "You're taking me to that stud farm, aren't you?"

He nodded. "I thought maybe we'd better get this out of your system. The Major and I inquired about those German horses but nobody seemed to know much about them down here. The owner, Mr. Boynton, is away you know. But they'll let us go through the stables. The Major fixed that for us."

The Maryland landscape was flatter than the hilly country they had left behind and it seemed that they went for miles between level, white-fenced pastures before they came to the sign that announced the Boynton Farms. The superintendent, a man named Hamish, remembered Neal and took them around himself. "I wouldn't do this for anyone but the Major," he said with a polite smile.

The stables were magnificent, almost as grand and every bit as well cared for as the stables at Kisber, Illi thought. Clearly a great deal of money had been spent

191

here, private money, too, and not government funds. They went from stall to stall exclaiming over the magnificent specimens of horseflesh housed there. In one building Mr. Hamish said, "We have here some stallions that we use for breeding hunters and riding horses, also racers for the lesser events, good horses but not big winners for one reason or another."

"Wild horses?" Illi asked.

"What do you know about wild horses?" Mr. Hamish asked in turn.

"I know there are such horses, thoroughbreds that the Jockey Club will not recognize," said Illi, showing off a bit.

Mr. Hamish looked at Neal over her head, raised his eyebrows, and smiled condescendingly. "Well, while some of our horses are not in the Stud Book they are all quite tame, I assure you," he said smoothly.

They went the rounds of the stalls while soulful eyes gazed at them incuriously and various snorts and neighs greeted them as Mr. Hamish handed out the sugar lumps he had brought along. Then they came to one stall door where the name plate hanging over it said *Gamester*.

Illi stopped suddenly and then dashed forward to look into the stall past the gold chestnut head with the star on the forehead, and the wide-spaced large eyes. Yes, the stallion had four white stockings!

Mr. Hamish put out a hand to pull her back. "Not too close," he said. "Gamester isn't vicious, but you never know what he's going to do."

"Gamester? That isn't his name. His name is Vidám," Illi said, speaking as if she were in a trance.

"Illi, are you sure? How can you be?" Neal asked.

"Of course I am sure. If you had not seen your brother or sister for eight years, you would know them again, would you not?" And in spite of Mr. Hamish's hand she went up close to Vidám to let him nuzzle her fingers. "See?" she said delightedly. "He remembers me."

"What is all this?" Mr. Hamish asked in a puzzled way.

"Miss Horvath has lost a horse," Neal explained, "and she thinks she has found him. Was this one of those Hungarian horses brought over here after the war?"

"You'd have to ask Mr. Boynton about that," Mr. Hamish said cautiously. "I wasn't here then. What was your idea, Miss Horvath? Are you going to try and claim him?"

"Oh no, I had not thought of that. I have no proof, have I? Only my heart knows and that does not count."

Mr. Hamish seemed to be relieved. "It's possible Mr. Boynton might be willing to sell him, at a price," he said.

"I am very much afraid I could not buy him, Mr. Hamish," Illi told him. "But just to know he is here, alive and safe, well cared for . . ." she turned away to hide the tears that had come to her eyes. Her back was to the stall. Vidám stretched his long neck and with a mischievous snort thrust his nose under the brim of her hat, gave it a flip that sent it falling off in front of her.

Illi whirled and holding out her hand to Mr. Hamish said, "Sugar, please! That was his old trick. I taught him to do that. You see, he does remember!"

Mr. Hamish seemed duly surprised as he watched Vidám take the sugar from her fingers. "I never saw him do that before, have you?" to the grinning stable boy who stood nearby.

"No suh, that horse is full of tricks but that ain't one of them."

"I'd like to try another, may I?" Illi asked Mr. Hamish. "Could you let him out in the paddock for a moment?"

Mr. Hamish motioned the boy to take Gamester from his stall. Outside Illi walked away for a little distance. Then she turned and said, "Now let him go." The boy dropped the halter, but the horse did not move. Then Illi cried, high and clear, "Vidám, *gyere ide!*" The horse came running and stopped dutifully before her, throwing back his forelock.

"You see?" she turned to Mr. Hamish. "That is part of my proof if I needed it."

The stable boy's eyes widened. "What did she say, boss? Is it a conjure?"

Neal laughed. "It's just Hungarian for 'Come here' and Vidám is his name. It means Happy-go-lucky," he said, enjoying the show.

"That's him. He's happy-go-lucky all right," said the boy, grinning now. "You want I should change the name, boss?"

"No, not yet," said Mr. Hamish and led the way back to his office. There he went to a shelf where he took down a large record book, leafing it through. "Yes," he said finally, "here it is: Gamester, 1947, five-year-old chestnut colt, bought from Mr. Lee Dubois, no papers, and then it's marked 'thoroughbred' with a question mark after it. That's all the history we have on him."

"It does not matter, I know," Illi said confidently. "Tell me one thing, Mr. Hamish, was Hocus-pocus his get?"

"Yes, I believe he was. That's the colt who went to Major Wallace, isn't it?"

"Yes." She turned to Neal. "You see, I was right, right, all the time about Pokey. No wonder I loved him. Mr. Hamish, would you mind very much if I went back alone to say good-by to Vidám?"

Mr. Hamish said he wouldn't mind and so she went alone to stand and whisper all kinds of things in Vidám's willing ear. "We're lucky, Vidám, you and I both, luckier than the rest of them, poor Grandfather, the Czernys, the others like them who had to go back to Hungary, and most of the poor, starved horses. We have found good homes, kind people. They may call us wild horses, but we both know it is only a name. It means nothing. Maybe we can see each other once in a while, Vidám, and remember the old days together."

On the way back home she sat so quietly that Neal was moved to ask in a worried way, "You in a stew over that horse, Illi? Because if you are, I'll be sorry I brought you down here."

"No," she said, "I'm just thinking."

"Not thinking of buying *him*? Fifty dollars wouldn't go very far on *that* deal."

Illi laughed self-consciously. "I know, Neal. I know now it wouldn't go far on any good horse. No, I realize I could never possess Vidám. But it does not seem to matter so much any more. I have other things to make me happy. I feel like a little girl who puts away her dolls."

"Glad to hear that," he said.

After that she began to sing. She sang all the way back home. Sometimes Neal joined her until she started on her Hungarian songs. "*Itt hagyon a falutokat,*" she sang, "Now I leave my little village, soon I will leave for a foreign country far, far away," fitting the English words to the plaintive Hungarian music for Neal's benefit.

"Are you really as sad as you sound?" he asked.

"Sad? Not really. It's a pleasant kind of sadness. I've told you that we Hungarians amuse ourselves with our tears. We cry with one eye and laugh with the other."

"Okay," he said and leaned over and kissed her cheek. "But let's act American for a while and laugh with *both* eyes. I like my girl better when she's laughing."

Chapter 18

IT WAS AN open winter in that part of the country, with only an occasional snow that did not last long enough to keep the ground covered. On sunny days when the ground was right Illi would hurry home from school and go straight to the Wallace stables where Tim or Jake would saddle Pokey while she slipped into her old jodhpurs which she kept in the tack room closet. There was not a minute to waste, for the winter days were short and Saturdays and Sundays would not be enough.

The jumps were kept set up in the small fenced pasture. Neal had said Pokey could already clear a better-than-three-foot hurdle, which was true, but he was still awkward. She worked with him to give him style in his jumping performance until his movements were smooth and rhythmical. The bar was moved up inch by inch but still kept loose in case he should nick it going over, which he sometimes did. He seemed to have developed a front tick in his left forefoot.

"That's easily corrected," Tim, one of the grooms, told her and went to lay another white rail on the ground a few feet beyond the jump. "Now watch. He may not jump wide enough to clear this at first, but he will when he gets on to the fact that he has to lift that front foot higher."

Several times they took a spill but Illi had learned to fall clear of the horse and was none the worse except for bruises which she bore bravely and secretly.

And so they went, over and over, until Pokey learned to lift that forefoot higher. The rail was raised gradually until he could clear the required three-foot-six and better. Then the rail was fastened so it would not topple if he kicked it. That went fine for a time and then suddenly he developed a hind tick.

Illi was discouraged. Neal was watching that day. He wasn't out often when she was working with Pokey and she had never asked for him. Her bargain with the Major had been made to relieve Neal of just this thing.

"Don't worry," he said. "We'll pole him a few times," and calling Tim they held a pole behind and below the jump. As Pokey came up to the railed fence, they waited until his body lifted to take it and they raised the pole to nudge his hind feet higher as a reminder. It took several times of this until he took the hint.

"He'll have his bad days," Neal said, "and you may have to repeat some of this training, but I don't think so.

Pokey's smart. He not only has good horse sense but he learns quickly. Keep at it, Illi, you're doing fine."

Illi kept at it. So did Neal in his way. Sometime in February he was given his physical examination in preparation for the West Point exams in March. He passed the physical with a good record.

"You see before you an excellent specimen of American manhood," he said importantly, flexing his muscles. "No glasses, no ear trumpets, no crutches. Now all they have to find out is whether the inside of my head is as good as the outside."

Illi, mounted on Pokey, looked down with the confidence she had shown all along. "If I were as sure of Pokey as I am of you, I wouldn't worry at all."

"How's he coming?"

"Fine. I have to watch his manners, though. He's so darn curious. He's like a little boy. He wants to see everything that is going on around him. I'm wondering if I can keep him still and at attention when he gets in the show. Tim says that is one of the points they will judge him on, obedience and manners."

And so the winter passed, all too quickly it seemed. March came and Neal went to Washington to take his exams. He was gone four days. It was a breathless time for all of them, the Major and Mrs. Austin, Illi and Ardis, and even Mark and the Enwrights.

Neal came over to see them the night when it was all over. He looked tired. "At last I can let down," he said. "The die is cast, the fat's in the fire, my fate is in the lap of the gods. So now I stop worrying."

"How was it?" Ardis asked.

"Not as bad as I thought it would be. The physical

199

was a cinch, and the aptitude test was fairly easy. My German came in handy. But I don't expect to get awfully high marks in the math. I'm no brain, but I think I have passed. There was only one question I didn't know at all. It was in English lit. But I did something else. I wrote all around it, but I admitted that I did not know the particular thing they asked. I didn't want to seem like a complete flop, but I didn't want them to think I was trying to bluff either."

Mr. Enwright who was listening with interest said, "That sounds sensible to me. Showed ingenuity and honesty at any rate. And maybe that's what they're looking for."

"Are you going back to Waverly, Neal?" Mark asked.

"Yes, the Major thinks I should. If I don't make the Point he wants me to go on to State and take up agriculture and animal husbandry."

"Would you mind that?" Mrs. Enwright asked.

"No, but I'd like to please the Major. He's been awfully good to me, to both of us. Mom says she has only known one man who was finer than he—my Dad."

Mrs. Enwright laughed. "Well, you'll soon be calling the Major Dad, won't you?"

Neal grinned. "Yep, in June and it's all right with me," he said and changed the subject.

As spring turned the landscape green Illi found herself away from home more and more. At first Ardis had been a bit sulky about Illi's absences. "I don't think it's that horse at all," she said one day when she was in a peevish spell. "I think it's Neal."

Illi's face showed the hurt Ardis' words had done to her. "Why, Ardis, I did not know you felt that way.

You know Neal is not himself these days. He's terribly jittery inside waiting for the report on his West Point tests. I don't see much of him. Besides, you know that I promised the Major to have Pokey in good form by May. I have to finish what I have started."

"Oh, never mind me," Ardis said carelessly, "I don't count any more," and went off to her room and closed the door. She was walking now every day, moving about the rooms without her chair. But it tired her and often she was in a bad mood like this. It worried Illi.

That evening she cornered Mrs. Enwright alone. "Tell me something honestly, *Mütterchen*," she said, "do you feel that I am neglecting Ardis? I'd stop schooling Pokey this minute if you think I should. The Major would understand."

Mrs. Enwright looked up from the desk where she was working on household accounts. "No, don't consider it, Illi. I told the Major it would be all right, because I thought it would be good for Ardis to be left to herself more at this stage. She's been spoiled like any sick child, but she's well enough to grow out of it now. She can't expect to be the center of attraction forever. In fact the doctor thinks it would be a good idea to send her to school next year. We've been considering giving her a year at Miss Latch's."

"It's going to be hard for her," Illi said. "But I think she has what it takes."

"I think so, too. She's in a bad humor today because she hasn't had a letter from Tom."

"Yes," Illi said, "she lives for them. I hope Tom won't let her down."

"I don't think he will if he can help it," Mrs. Enwright said. "Just hope and pray nothing happens to him. I'm very fond of Tom Grimm. I couldn't ask for a nicer boy for a son if they both feel the same when the time comes. But it may be a long way off and we'll have to be patient with Ardis without giving her her way too much."

And so Illi went back to Pokey with a lighter heart. She tried to tell Ardis more about it to keep her interested. Then one day Mr. Enwright stopped the car on the way home from the hospital and Ardis was able to stand at the fence and watch Pokey and Illi in action. She was alive with excitement when Illi came home tired enough to flop into the first soft chair.

"I had no idea, Illi, what it takes to do that," she said. "You're wonderful with that horse, so understanding and so patient. How can you do it over and over and over?"

"It's just like anything else you want to do well," Illi said with a tired smile. "You practice scales on the piano over and over and you bang a tennis ball against a wall over and over for a good backhand, and you rip out the hem of a skirt and do it over and over. Have you heard from Tom?"

"Yes. He's at an airbase in Greenland now. I bet he hates it. He doesn't like the cold. But he never says so in his letters."

"Tom would never complain," Illi said. "I think Tom Grimm is an ace even if he is not a flier. And I think you are a very lucky girl, Ardis."

"Yes," Ardis said thoughtfully, "I know I am. And every day I know it more. I'm going to ask Daddy or Mark to take me over to watch you often. May I?"

"No reason why not. Pokey has to get used to an audience."

In April Mrs. Enwright took Illi into the city with her one day and had her outfitted for good riding clothes. "We can't shame Pokey with you in a hand-me-down outfit," she said.

They came home with gabardine breeches and a tweed jacket in a warm, soft tan, waistcoat and riding shirts, a stock and string gloves, and a little black velvet hat to set on top of Illi's blond curls. When she had seen the prices, Illi had insisted upon using her own money as far as it would go and Mrs. Enwright had let her. She felt justifiably proud as she strutted before the family after dinner that night in her new outfit.

Mark let out a wolf call of appreciation. "No one is going to watch Pokey with this apparition on his back," he said. "I just hope the judges prefer blondes with blue eyes and a figure that looks well in pants."

"So do I," said a voice from the doorway and Illi swung around to see Neal staring at her with a sort of wonderment.

"Why are you looking like that?" she blurted out in her confusion. "Haven't you ever seen a girl in riding togs before?"

"Not this girl." He came into the room greeting the others with his usual banter.

"She's a knockout, isn't she?" Mark said with a wink for Neal.

"Sure thing. I'm afraid Pokey hasn't a chance. Everyone will be looking at the girl on his back."

"Stop your joking, Neal," she said, but her heart was singing at the look in his eyes. "Can't you be serious a moment?"

"I'm serious right now. I have news. I come as the bearer of good tidings." He swept them a little bow. "You are gazing at one of the latest appointments of the President of the United States to the great and powerful West Point where they turn raw kids like me into officers of the Army—and gentlemen."

They clustered around to read the important letter he waved toward them and to shake his hand and call him Major and General Austin, to ask a hundred questions.

"Do you really get paid for going to school?" Ardis asked.

"Yes, but by the time we pay for our uniforms and books and things there isn't much left. But we don't get much chance to spend money—not at first anyway."

"Don't you get any vacations?"

"The three upper classmen do in the summer but the poor plebes have to sweat it out there."

"Then we'll have to come and see you, won't we?" Illi said.

"Some day you're going to look up from greasing a gun and see Illi prancing up on Pokey across the parade ground," Mark teased.

Neal laughed. "I'll settle for letters, big ones, and often," he said.

In the next few weeks Illi thought Neal was a different person. She had never really realized what fun he could be. Now all the inner stress that he had tried to cover with a casual good-humor was gone. He was really sure of himself. And she saw him almost every day for he had taken on the schooling of Pokey, giving her additional pointers, grooming Pokey himself until his coat shone like satin.

And then the big day came. The Major had entered Pokey in the Green Hunter Lightweight Class. He explained the rules of the show to Illi carefully.

"It's all very complicated to me," Illi told Neal later. "I've never even been to a horse show before."

"Don't worry. I'll be right there in the paddock. All you have to do is ride Pokey, and get him a ribbon if you can. I don't think the Major expects too much of him at this time. He's as new at shows as you are."

She hoped Pokey was not feeling as much stage fright as she was as she waited outside the ring for the jumping order to be arranged at the gate. On her back was a big number, 23. Pokey was behaving beautifully so far, a little restless, especially when the band started up between events.

She looked out over the grandstand with its flying banners, to the milling crowds, the intent spectators lined along the rail watching the three-gaited saddle horse event, the youngsters with their cones and their spun-sugar candy, people in casual but expensive sports clothes, and other people in cheap finery, the cars lined up close to the grounds with people swarming all over them, even on the roofs, and she thought it was not unlike a country fair or a horse race at home. How often Janni and she had stood like the children here, each holding a hand of Grandfather Laszlos, watching with held breaths while the beautiful Hungarian thoroughbreds flashed by! Janni had the true Hungarian's love for good horses. He had a much better way with them than she had. He should be working with horses now instead of skis. If he were only here!

She tried to put all such ideas away from her as she

spotted the station wagon and saw Ardis waving to her. But she did not wave back. She was remembering her manners, even though she was not yet in the ring. It was a grave occasion.

"You're fifth, Illi," she heard Neal say. "Don't get nervous. Just take it easy and let Pokey take over. He won't fail you."

But Illi wasn't listening. She was watching the eighth horse waiting to enter the ring. It was a beautiful black mare and Peachy was riding her, Peachy in hunt costume and looking very much at ease.

One by one she watched the riders on their beautiful hunters enter the ring, collect their horses, and send them at the jumps, first the post and rail, then the brush, and lastly the white board fence. One young hunter refused a jump and another knocked the rail with a fore-foot, both serious faults, as Illi had been told.

Then it was Illi's turn and Pokey and she were off. She forgot everything then except the task of the moment. It was the same as it had been in the Major's pasture. Pokey's rhythm was something one could sing to. She felt him gather himself for the first jump and leaned forward for the lift. He was over. Then the brush and he cleared that too. The fence—would he balk here? "Please, Pokey," she whispered and without a second's break he had cleared it well. But was that a tick she heard behind her or was it just a noise from the crowd?

"Wonderful!" Neal cried, running to meet her as she left the ring. "Perfect as far as I could see. You'll have to go through it again if it is, most likely. They have to eliminate, you know."

But Illi wasn't listening. She was watching that eighth

horse enter the ring. Peachy had scarcely flicked an eye as she passed Neal and Illi. Now Illi threw the reins to Tim and ran to the rail to watch. The black mare came through beautifully and Illi could feel her stomach turning over at the thought of competing with such a professional show as Peachy had put on.

"Oh dear!" she sighed.

"What are you oh-dearing about?" Neal asked as he came to stand beside her.

"Because I'll never be able to ride like that," she said in honest appreciation.

"How do you know? You can't see yourself. I think the Major is going to be very proud of you, even if you don't get a ribbon out of it."

Illi smiled and went to find Tim who was leading the blanketed Pokey around the paddock.

"How is he?" she asked.

"Fresh as a daisy. That's what I told Miss Prentice."

"Miss Prentice?"

"Yes. She's mad as hops about something. Says Pokey should be disqualified. Says she thought this show was for Americans, not foreigners."

"What?" Illi gasped. "But, it's the Major's horse and certainly he is American enough."

"That's what I told her," said Tim. "But she's furious all right. Wouldn't even speak to Mr. Neal."

From the twelve entries in the event only seven were asked to repeat. Number 23 was third, and Peachy sixth. Again Pokey and Illi took the course and again emerged fault free. And again Illi watched Peachy on the black mare. He was not behaving well. Illi guessed he had caught the mood of his rider whose cheeks were crimson with controlled anger. He cleared the rail and the brush jumps but at the fence something happened. He seemed to become confused and to everyone's surpise he refused the jump. Peachy wheeled him around and back to try again. This time he took it but the damage was done.

"Looks like he did it on purpose," Tim said, waiting beside her. "Too bad. I think his rider fouled him up."

Five horses were assembled in the center of the ring waiting for the jump-off now for the ribbons. This time Pokey was first. His performance was as good as ever. He seemed to be enjoying himself, his muscles performing like clockwork, but as they approached the fence something white fluttered over the rail and for a moment Illi thought Pokey was going to break his pace.

She went weak with fright and she might have fallen if she had not been holding so tight to Pokey's reins. Then she got herself in hand, remembering where she was and that only one thing was important—to get Pokey over that last jump. As if he knew what she was thinking Pokey took the fence with such nonchalance that the crowd cheered.

She went back to the center of the ring to wait, straight in the saddle, eyes front, her hands on the reins holding the restless Pokey. The judges took a long time. The jumping over, they went up and down the line now ranged head to tail, making notes in their little books. There was a short conference and the five were lined up in a different order, but Illi was still first. She tried not to look too pleased nor surprised when she went up to take the blue ribbon that was handed to her.

The Major rushed out to greet her after she had ridden around the ring to the applause of the crowd, and she could hardly see his big, tweed-clad figure for her tears.

"Why, Illi, you're crying," he said, helping her from the horse. "Did anything happen?"

"Don't mind her, Major," Neal said coming up to them. He put an arm across her shoulder enthusiastically. "Don't you know a true Hungarian always cries when she is happy?"

"But I'm not a true Hungarian any more," she said, wiping away a tear with the back of her glove. "I belong to a fine American family now, you know."

"And some day you'll be marrying an officer in the American Army, don't forget that," Neal said for her ears alone, as the Major walked away. They stood looking at each other while the crowd milled around them. Yes, some day she'd be married to Neal if she was lucky and he didn't fall in love with somebody else.

"Oh, Neal," she said impulsively, "I wish you weren't going away for four long years."

"Now, now," he said, poking a curl back under her black velvet cap, "where's the girl who said she could 'stick around' for four years? You've got to, Illi. I'm counting on that."

She nodded. "I'll stick," she said. "And I'll write you every day." She smiled up at him happily and tucked her arm in his as they sauntered over to the station wagon where the rest had gathered, Mr. and Mrs. Enwright, Ardis, Mark, Geegee, the Major, and Mrs. Austin.

"Illi," the Major boomed in his big voice, "I've been hearing all about your brother. You'll have to give me his address. I'll be needing a new right-hand man when

Neal goes away, and if there is any way of getting him over here I'd like to give that Janni of yours a job."

"When Neal goes away," Ardis repeated. "I hate to hear you say that, Major. It won't be long now, will it, Neal?"

"Nope, six weeks."

"We'll miss you," Mrs. Enwright said.

"Not as much as I will," Neal's mother said.

"But don't forget, Mom, I've got a replacement." Neal winked at the Major. "That right, Pop?"

"That's right. I'm counting on you for best man in June."

Ardis let out an extravagant sigh. "What a day *this* has turned out to be!" she exclaimed. "A winning horse, and a wedding coming up. I don't know when I've been so excited."

"But the best thing of all is to see you standing there without your wheel chair," Illi said, her voice brimming with love for Ardis and all of them. Then she realized that she had been crushing something over and over in her hand. It was Pokey's blue ribbon. "Oh dear," she said handing it to the Major. "I forgot to give you this. Or should I have pinned it on Pokey?"

The Major took the ribbon and examined it for a moment thoughtfully. Then he looked around at the others who were all looking at the flushed, blonde girl in the smart riding costume. There was love, admiration, and honest pride in the eyes of all of them.

"I think from all I have been hearing lately," he said, clearing his throat of a sudden huskiness, "that this ribbon belongs rightly to you, my dear." He made a short ceremonious bow and pinned it on Illi's lapel. "A blue for Illi Horvath, for a girl who has overcome more things than brush jumps and rail fences, a girl who has come out a champion."

Again Illi's eyes filled with tears and she threw herself into Mrs. Enwright's arms sobbing, "Oh, *Mütterchen*, I'm so happy, so happy. But it's *you* who should have the ribbon, it's you who put up with me."

"Of course," said the Major with a twinkle in his eyes, "if you want to give the ribbon away you can give it to Pokey. It will be keeping it in the family, because I'm giving you the little horse, Illi. You've earned him."

"Giving me Pokey?" She could not believe her ears.

"I couldn't very well sell him when he was a gift to me, could I?" the Major asked comically. "That's what I told Peachy Prentice just this afternoon. I think it up-set her a bit."

"But—but don't you want him yourself?" Illi asked.

"No, I've got to get rid of him. I've got a lot of foals coming along and I need the stable room. So he's yours. I can't imagine anyone I'd rather see have him. I'm just sorry there are no papers to go with him."

"Papers, what are papers?" Illi scoffed. "He's just as good a horse without papers, even if they do call him a 'wild horse.'" She began to laugh. "I guess you could call me a 'wild horse' too. I haven't much to show in the way of credentials."

"But you're a thoroughbred just the same," Neal said, squeezing her arm.

Illi went up to the Major and held out her hand. "I don't know how to thank you," she said earnestly. "You are so generous, you are all so generous. I think Americans are the most generous people in the world. And now if you'll excuse me, please, I would like to go and tell Pokey that he belongs to me."

She crossed the paddock to the stables, scarcely conscious of the admiring faces along the rail. She was thinking of all the day had brought forth. She had so much to be thankful for, Pokey who now belonged to her, Neal's appointment, Janni's job that the Major would bring about somehow, and Ardis' slow but sure recovery. She wished she could go off by herself, just she and Pokey who had come to nuzzle her fingers as if he knew everything that had happened.

She put her cheek against his soft nose and began to whisper things to him until a step stopped behind her and she turned to find Neal watching her.

"I want to get into the act," he said, throwing his arm around her shoulders and giving her a little squeeze. "How about it, Pokey?"

Pokey gave a slight whinny and then a moist white nose was thrust between them, pushing them apart.

"Why, Pokey," Illi cried, laughing, "I believe you're jealous."

"It's okay, old boy," Neal said, digging into his pocket for a piece of sugar. "I'll treat her all right, I swear I will. And I'll let you have her all to yourself for four long years."

Pokey gave out another low whinny and backed discreetly away as if he were well pleased with the whole situation.

Wisconsin State College at Eau Claire
LIBRARY RULES

No book should be taken from the library until it has been properly charged by the librarian.

Books may be kept one week but are not to be renewed without special permission of the librarian.

A fine of two cents a day will be charged for books kept over time.

In case of loss or injury the person borrowing this book will be held responsible for a part or the whole of the value of a new book.

Due	DUE	Due	DUE
Apr 23			
May 2			
Nov 5			
Nov 2			
Sep 16 63			
Oct 16			
MAY 27 '65			
APR 26 '67			